Unbridled Steele

Unbridled Steele

A WOMEN OF STAMPEDE NOVEL

NICOLE ROY

Published 2018 by Nicole Roy

ISBN: 978-1-7752046-0-2 (Print edition)

Design and cover art by Su Kopil, Earthly Charms
Copyediting by Ted Williams

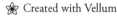 Created with Vellum

DEDICATION

To my Mom. Who is my rock.
I love you, Mom.

And to my Negymama, who encouraged me to write,
to live in love and who will never be forgotten.

ACKNOWLEDGMENTS

There are so many people who helped me complete this book. My friends for supporting me and putting up with me. My beta readers for giving me their time, their opinions and their wise insights, and to my family who didn't choose me, but got stuck loving me.

I would like to deeply thank Shelley Kassian, Katie O'Connor and Brenda Sinclair for their generous spirit and guidance through the whole process, without them I would be a deer in the headlights and without them, this book would literally never have been completed.

PREFACE

I would like to offer my humblest apologies if I have written any part of the Western world in error. I have the utmost respect for the history and strength of the Western culture in Alberta and wanted to honor it.

I hope you enjoy Unbridled Steele and can feel my love of the Calgary Stampede and the great city of Calgary.

CHAPTER 1

*S*arah Steele heard the anxious bawling of cattle and the excited whooping shouts of men. "What the hell?" Her brows furrowed as she trotted her horse over the grassy hill. She reached over the pommel of the saddle and patted Nigel on his smooth brown neck. They had spent the whole day in the hot summer sun of the Alberta foothills chasing the last of the scattered herd. She wasn't impressed to come back to their staging area in the large green clearing to a commotion.

The green prairie stretched out before her, defining the end of the foothills. In the meadow below a herd of cattle clustered into a temporary pen. They should have been munching on lush grasses and salts, but their large brown bodies were moving in an agitated cluster. The XYZ brand on their thighs still marked perfectly straight lines; clean and easy to read. Satisfied the cattle were accounted for and for the most part okay, she swung her gaze across the field.

The other workers, who had apparently finished their work early, were standing around an old wooden fence that formed a pen for one of the herding corrals. Sarah listened to angry, huffing grunts from an enormous stallion, that and the men's hollering. A large wild horse trotted in a tight circle of the pen. It was clearly agitated. A beautiful equine with white patches dotting his legs and streaking across his face.

"They aren't gunna try to ride that horse, are they?" Sarah's friend, Becca stood in the saddle to see what was going on. They were too far away to see exactly what the commotion was, but the unnatural noises were enough to make their horses step uncomfortably.

"Nigel." Sarah's soothing tones and relaxed posture worked to keep the muscled beast under her calm, but she could see Becca's younger pinto shifting and twitching uneasily. "They're idiots," Sarah said, cocking her head at the group of men. "They're spooking the cows."

Becca shrugged. "What can you do? Men will often be idiots."

The cattle they had spent the day rounding up, were vocalizing their anxiety, and Sarah would be damned if she allowed her hard day's work to be foolishly undone by some rowdy cowboys.

"Maybe," she said, "but Steeles will always be Steeles." She made a clicking sound and gently tapped Nigel with her feet. He responded fluidly and cantered across the grassy field towards the cowboys.

"Hey!" Sarah yelled to the group the second she was within earshot. A few heads snapped towards her at the commanding tone but some workers on the other side continued to holler at the stallion. The stable hands were smart enough to get out of her way. It gave her a clear view of the stallion in the ring. He was gorgeous. His trot announced his wild heritage and free spirit. He whinnied and stomped and picked up his pace, tossing his head, his light mane flowing behind him. Sarah was mesmerized by the majesty of the horse, but then a cowboy entered the ring and he snagged her attention. He was broader in the shoulder than most cowboys, with obvious strength in his bare arms and thick muscles running down his thighs. His slightly bowlegged gait was classic cowboy; so was his black Stetson, tight-fitted jeans and short-sleeved blue plaid shirt. His bullheaded egotism had Sarah frowning as he ran in a tight circle beside the wild stallion.

Who the hell did this guy think he was?

Sarah's eyes were glued to what was happening in the ring. She knew better than to intervene. She didn't like what was going on, but she still respected that a man was in a relatively small space with a wild animal. She cast a quick glance behind her, at the herd of cattle mooing and milling about in the field. They were shifting uneasily but were staying put for the moment.

Twisting back, she watched the bold cowboy approach the horse, held her breath as he increased his stride, and glared as he began to run and keep pace. His voice was low and soothing though Sarah couldn't make out what he was saying. An odd flutter stirred in the pit of her stomach as she watched him. His smooth stride and confidence were wholly misplaced. Did the man not see the agitation broiling inside the stallion; the quiver in the barrel chest? The shine in the wild eyes?

His hand grasped the light blonde mane of the tall stallion and he threw his leg over the horse's back hauling his body to land on top. Sarah watched him land squarely on the broad horse, and her stomach turned as he was bolted forward and jarred harshly back, the horse jumping and bucking. The cowboy's spectators cheered their idiotic encouragement, which echoed with the increasing commotion from the cattle to make a near-deafening chorus. She watched as the stallion hurled forward, leaping in the air, trying to dislodge the human from his back. One frenzied move and the cowboy lost his grip, his body flung backwards off the side of the horse. He hit the ground with a heavy thump, landing on his back, his legs followed to crumple on top, like a slinky that suddenly stopped slinking. Dust blew out from under him. The cheers of the surrounding men didn't drown out the painful grunt that burped out of the man on the ground.

The stallion wasn't done. The sharp flick of tail and rough look in his eye had Sarah reaching for her lasso.

The cowboys were suddenly quiet now, each realizing the danger, but all were motionless as they watched the cowboy struggle to stand. The stallion stomped the ground and charged.

Sarah sharply squeezed Nigel as she maneuvered the rough rope. Her horse sprang forward as the lasso circled over her head. She wrapped the loose end around the horn of her saddle as she let the loop fly.

A fraction of a satisfied smile cocked her lips as the rope circled over the shoulders of the dazed cowboy.

She yanked on the lasso and watched as it snugged around his shoulders, then she kicked her booted feet and yelled, "heayaw." Nigel responded instantly and lunged backwards.

The lasso tightened as Sarah's clever horse jumped back, hauling the cowboy's body sideways, just barely pulling him out of the way of the charging stallion, whose bared teeth and aggressive charge made his intent clear.

The stallion ran through the now empty space, huffing and stomping his feet. The cowboy's body dragged like a sack of potatoes over the ground; with his arms pinned to his sides, he was helpless in trying to protect himself. She couldn't see his face, but he would be a little winded from the sudden jerk of her lasso, which was a better choice than being crushed by a wild horse.

Sarah quickly untwisted the lasso off the horn of her saddle and threw it to the ground, freeing the cowboy. She called Nigel to a trot and backed him up into the pen, which took a little extra encouraging as the wild stallion was still bucking and huffing inside. "Yaw!" Sarah hollered. She pulled on the reins, jabbed her heels into Nigel's side and leaned forward. Nigel lifted his muscled legs to kick at the boards of the temporary corral. Sarah watched two of the planks fall to the ground. Hopefully that would be enough.

She looked over her shoulder at the wild stallion, his dark eyes lighting up at the fence opening.

It was enough.

Sarah loosened her hold on Nigel's reins and leaned forward. "Yeah!" she hollered again, her body leaning far over the pummel, hugging the horse's neck as she slackened the reins. Nigel needed no further encouragement. Sarah hung onto the horn as Nigel's solidly muscled body leaped from standing to a fullout canter in two seconds flat. He loved to run and was happy to kick into high gear as he tore across the field. Sarah looked behind her to ensure her plan had worked. The stallion had seen the opening in the fence, as she had hoped, and had jumped over the fallen planks to follow the running horse across the field. Herd mentality took over as he raced after Nigel.

Sarah saw the cowboy pull off her lasso as the other men circled around him. He stood firmly, his feet wide apart as he watched her ride away. Her hat flew off, her long black hair breaking free of the loose braid to tangle into wild disarray. She didn't care. Her thighs clung to the worn leather saddle as her horse flew over the green spring hills. She turned forward, letting the wind fly over her face and whip her hair off her cheeks and forehead. The low bellows of the cattle grew softer as she galloped into the distance, and her heart beat happily as the stallion ran next to her and Nigel, shaking his large head and kicking up his feet.

For a second, she wished she was on Starbuck. She had trained the young thoroughbred since it had learned to walk. She had taken Sarah into the championship circle many times while barrel racing. Thinking of Starbuck's amazing speed, and how thrilling it would have been to be riding her alongside the wild stallion sent a shot of yearning through Sarah.

Starbuck would have given the stallion a genuine run for his money. The canter and speed of Nigel, a quarter horse bred for life on a ranch and owned by Sarah, was nothing compared to the grace and cadence of Starbuck. This horse was owned by the Letters End Ranch, and though Sarah worked there and was able to train and ride all the horses, she did not own this phenomenal animal. Starbuck had been bred for speed and agility and her lineage could be traced to the sultans of Arabia. She was meant for a better life than running in the woods or rounding up cattle. Sarah could never afford such a magnificent animal.

Nigel was an amazing horse, loyal and strong and she felt bad for thinking of Starbuck. She leaned into the wind, enjoying the moment.

Sarah allowed Nigel to run until the trees came into view. She decreased his speed until he was trotting gently. The stallion had kept pace the entire ride, but now continued toward the woods, trotting closer to the wilderness, his withers foamy from the run, his eyes holding an alert glassiness and his panting emitting in huffy breaths. She had to pull on the reins slightly harder than usual to encourage Nigel to stop. She was sure he felt the exhilaration of running with the stallion as much as she did. But it was time to head back to the trucks. There were horses to load, chores to do, and an arrogant cowboy to deal with.

She watched the stallion until he disappeared into the forest. She sighed deeply and headed back to the trailers.

The small wooden pen now had no spectators, even the broken board had been replaced. The workers were packing up the horses, putting out chop for the cows and loading the trailers. The cattle were calm and content.

She scanned the workers but didn't see the cowboy in the blue plaid anywhere. Maybe he had left already.

She rode Nigel slowly through the trailers and trucks, inspecting the area to ensure things were done correctly and to her standard.

"Peter," she called to a worker, "don't forget to put Rowdy and Sam in the same stall tonight," she reminded him, and was satisfied with his eager nod.

"Not too much chop for those heifers, Curtis." She pointed to the animals getting their grains and oats. "They'll get more tomorrow." The young cowboy eased up on pouring the food into the troughs.

"Troy, if you forget to idle that truck down again, you are on chicken coop duty for a month." The young kid ran to do as he was told.

Sarah waved to Becca, who was talking with a few workers at her truck, but when they saw her coming they broke up the chatting and went to work again.

Once she made it to her horse trailer and truck, Sarah swung her leg over the saddle and jumped off.

"What the hell was that!" The cowboy came out of nowhere the second she dismounted.

Up close, he was more than she expected. He was taller than her, and built like a "Y", broad in the shoulder, flat in the stomach with thick long legs that rooted him to the ground. Seeing him from a distance did not prepare her for the up-close striking image of the man now. He had black hair peeking out from under his fancy black hat, with dark stubble on his face. His lean features were handsome and rugged. Sarah gazed at him, twice. There was something vaguely familiar about him, tugging at the corner of her mind.

He wore a loose long-sleeved red plaid shirt and tight, dark jeans that hugged his thighs and widened at his cowboy boots. She didn't miss the overly large belt buckle with the chiseled image of a bucking bull and a rider firmly on top.

Figures he would be a bull rider.

Sarah glanced at his face. He glared at her furiously, his dark brown eyes appearing light next to his dark hair. The familiarity struck her again. "Do I know you?"

"Oh, yeah, we met earlier." His thumb jutted towards the empty pen.

"What exactly is your problem?" she demanded, not cowed by his misplaced anger. She'd probably saved his life.

"You lassoed me?! Who lassoes people!" He sputtered.

"Who jumps into a pen with a wild animal like that, with the cattle there?" she countered.

"I have some experience riding."

"You've barebacked wild stallions, have you?"

He scowled.

"I don't know who brought you to help with the roundup, but we won't need you next year." She turned dismissively to unsaddle Nigel.

Letters End Ranch was a large working stable and farm with many employees, but during busy times it was not uncommon to have extra people to help during roundup and branding. But this guy was obviously too arrogant for common sense and Sarah did not tolerate his particular mix of anger, ignorance and conceit.

"What? Not welcome? Why? The stallion was fine. I just rode him."

"I know, I was there." Sarah loosened the sweaty cinch and hauled off the saddle and blanket. She grabbed Nigel's brush. "From where I was sitting, you were bucked off a wild stallion." She came around Nigel's left side to brush his damp coat.

"That's how you dismount."

"And," she said, ignoring his stupid statement, "you were about to get crushed, trampled, and stomped on by that stallion."

The cowboy didn't reply, so Sarah continued. "Your back was to him, he was running at you. If I hadn't pulled you out of the way, I would be putting you in an ambulance. Instead of putting up with your attitude."

He scoffed. Which wasn't surprising; no one liked being told they did something wrong. Sarah turned, giving him her full attention. "Do you hear those cows?" She paused for effect, the cries of the younger calves mixed with the upset of the older ones. "I know you didn't hurt the stallion, but your idiotic behavior unnecessarily disturbed the herd. I don't know what you were trying to prove, or who you were trying to impress, but there is more to a round up than ten second satisfaction and an ego trip. More to think about than just one cowboy. Your behavior was irresponsible. The stallion is fine. The herd is fine. And you, whether you like it or not, have been dealt with."

The cowboy scowled.

"So now you have a choice," Sarah continued, "you can cowboy-up and say 'thank you' or prove my point and choose to be an asshole."

His eyes rounded, and the muscle in his jaw flexed, but no words came out. She waited another few seconds, giving him ample time to form a response. When he didn't speak, she flashed a smug, insincere smile. "See," she said, her smile dropping, "I'm hardly ever wrong."

She had to brush the other side of Nigel, but the cowboy stood in her way. She was about to continue her diatribe when she noticed something "Weren't you wearing a different shirt?" The question popped out of her mouth before she gave it much thought.

He glanced down at his shirt, like he had forgotten what he was wearing. His cowboy hat tipped, hiding his face. When he faced her again his cheeks were flushed.

"You dragged me through horse shit, so I had to change."

Sarah blinked at him; she was able to hold her expression blank and perfectly still for all of two seconds before a smile threatened to appear. She held her lips down, trying not to grin, but thinking about his indignation of being lassoed, and then dragged through the natural occurrence of a roundup was a little too much. She snickered, failing to hide her smirk as a bubble of laughter escaped her lips.

The look on his face didn't help. Sarah chuckled, bending over with the effect and leaning back again.

"It really isn't that funny," he grumbled.

She laughed a little harder.

"Sarah!" A familiar baritone voice called her name.

"Hey, Bruce." She tried to squash her laughter as her boss approached them. His pristine six horse trailer was already hooked up to his King Ranch truck, his horses had been loaded by the workers. Sarah could see Duke sitting in the cab, his long dog tongue drooping out his panting lips. Bruce's thin legs carried his tall barrel-chested frame towards her in an off-kilter strut.

"You all loaded?" she asked, blinking away a few tears from laughing.

"Almost. Are you coming back to Letters End for steaks and beer?"

Sarah smiled. "Wouldn't miss it."

"Great, so you have room in your truck."

"Yeah, why?"

"I was going to introduce you, but I see you've already met Laine." Bruce waved his hand to the cowboy.

The name triggered her memory and it suddenly hit her. "Laine Young, the CPRA bull rider? The three-time world champ!?" *No way.*

"The one and only." Bruce's tone sounded like he was announcing something at a carnival.

"I'm not *just* a bull rider," Laine muttered.

Sara heard Laine's resentment; but Bruce continued talking.

"Laine is also with the Blaser Investment Group."

Sarah's mouth popped open in shock. She snapped it shut and blinked the surprise from her eyes.

"So, you…" she trailed off, afraid to speak the sentence into fruition.

"Laine's company bought majority shares in Letters End," Bruce clarified.

"So, you own…" Sarah looked at the cowboy. His expression was unreadable.

"Laine, Sarah is the barrel racer I told you about. We're getting ready for her to compete in the Stampede. I tell ya, she jockeys those horses to amazing speeds, probably gunna break some records. She is also the top hand at the ranch and trains and works with, well…" Bruce looked to Sarah, "…most, if not, all, of the horses stabled with us. In fact, her grandmother was the first Calgary Stampede winner from Letters End…" Bruce trailed off, smiling broadly. When neither Sarah nor Laine spoke, he added: "Well, I'll leave you both to it, then." He turned his lanky form away. "Thanks for giving Laine a ride back to the ranch," he called over his shoulder.

Bruce had really shit timing.

Sarah stared at Laine, evaluating him with fresh eyes. Bruce had been talking about the investment group for months now. She understood that the ranch was a business, had always been corporately owned. First the Canadian government, then a series of investment groups and affluent business men. But even after all these years, the investors had left Bruce to make decisions and be the foreman of Letters End Ranch, managing the sale of horses, cows and grains and dealing with the day-to-day payroll and budgets. Which left her as the lead hand, running and deciding the intricacies of the ranch on her own. And for years the ranch had been successful, still was successful. She didn't like the way things were changing. That her work may be for nothing. Not now that this investor, this angry cowboy's opinion suddenly mattered.

This guy was supposedly going to invest thousands of dollars to move Letters End into the future, or so Bruce had told her. She didn't understand why the ranch had to move into any future. It was run with the routine and tradition of a hundred years. Forging the Alberta Western culture cow by cow and bale by bale. Hell, her grandparents had met working on the ranch, and her grandmother had worked there until last year. Sarah cut off her train of thought. She didn't want to dwell on that particular sorrow right now. She glared at the cowboy. Steeles had put their blood sweat and tears into Letters End; it felt cheap that they needed extra investors now.

It annoyed her enough to turn a polite question into a sneer as well as a snarky comment. "You need a ride?" But Laine just stared at her, his expression unreadable.

She was sweaty and dirty, which probably meant she had mud

on her face. She knew she smelled like horse, and cow and sunscreen. Her dark, almost black hair was a massive shoulder length tangle. So, what the hell was he staring at?

Shaking her head, she ignored him and loaded Nigel, then began hooking up her trailer. The old crank squeaked as she yanked on the lever. She cast a quick glance to Laine who was watching the other trucks and trailers pull off the field.

Sarah jumped in her truck, started up her old diesel and threw it into reverse. She leaned halfway out her window and looked behind her, hitting the pedal and easing off the clutch. Her truck lurched backwards at an odd angle. Laine jumped back, though the truck was nowhere close to him. He looked like he wanted to yell at her, or glare at her, or say something, but he stood watching, his brow furrowed.

She had backed up her old pickup so many times she was certain she could do it in the dark with her eyes closed. She had perfectly parked the ball hitch right under the pin. Sarah didn't break stride as she jumped from the truck and passed him again. She locked up the hitch, put the safety chains on, plugged in the trailer lights and headed back to the driver's door.

He was a world class bull rider; which was slightly intimidating on its own. But above that, he was an investor, and apparently had a lot of money tied up in the ranch. Which meant that he had a lot of money invested in the horse she had painstakingly trained and planned to ride for the Calgary Stampede. Purchased for 20K, Starbuck was an expensive little filly, and that didn't include the stable and feed costs, as well as vet checkups and shoeing. If he pulled funding… Sarah ignored the thought.

"You comin' or what?" she asked as she strode past him.

He hesitated for a second, his gaze taking in the quickly emptying field. He strode around the trailer to the passenger side. This was going to be a long ride.

CHAPTER 2

*L*aine was not in the mood to deal with this cowgirl right now. No, he couldn't even call her that. She was something else altogether and quite frankly he didn't know if he liked it. He kept his mouth shut and glared out the windshield.

She maneuvered the old Dodge slowly off the bumpy field. Her long legs shifting to release the clutch. Her dusty hand gripping and sliding the ball of the stick shift into gear. Her narrow shoulders twisted so she could keep an eye on the horse and trailer behind them.

He couldn't place why he didn't like her. She obviously knew what she was doing. The way she freed the wild stallion and rode into the wilderness was nothing short of awe-inspiring. Of course, he saw it sideways from the damn ground, but still. Inspiring. She had loaded up her horse and backed up her trailer like a pro, not asking for or needing his help in the slightest. She was competent. She was capable. He had spent the day with the workers from Letters End and every single one of them spoke highly and respectfully about her, yet she had him gritting his teeth.

"You done stewing over there? Or you wanna pout all the way

back to the ranch?" Sarah asked as the truck bumped along the gravel road.

There it was. He glared at her. Her directness was off-putting. She called it like she saw it. "I'm not pouting." He wished he'd said it with less sulkiness in his tone.

He crossed his arms over his chest. Damn it. This was not going like he wanted. Getting involved in Letters End was supposed to be a new start. A way to change the image and expectation of the 'jock bull rider'. He'd seen that look a thousand times. The typical one second size-up, the quick assumption that he was nothing more than what people assumed. And he couldn't begrudge her that. He did have a reputation.

But he wanted something more out of life and had wanted to start fresh. He hated falling into old habits; and riding the wild stallion had seemed like fun, so he'd jumped at the chance to show off. He wasn't proud of that. And to have her call him out on it; on his ego, and pride, especially when those were things he was determined to change, was incredibly maddening. He thought of his brutal divorce. Of the unexpected funeral he had attended for his best friend that had shocked him with its suddenness. Of the hundreds of 'one second size-ups' he was determined to stop getting.

If he wanted change, he would have to change. He uncrossed his arms. He inhaled and readjusted his hat, then turned to the woman driving. Bruce said she was the best jockey and trainer this side of the border. Laine didn't doubt it. He let his eyes wander over her dirty, jean-clad body.

She cranked down the window. The cool air shifted the dust in the truck and pulled at the loose strands of her hair. She rested her elbow on the window ledge and glanced at Laine, her lower lip between her teeth.

He reminded himself that he wanted to be a better person, that he wanted to make better choices. He didn't want to continue making mistakes in his life. And he knew that if he was going to succeed at the ranch, he would have to be amicable with the lead hand.

He could tell something was on her mind. But when she didn't speak he filled the silence. "So, do you lasso people often?" Laine asked, employing a casual, non-pouty tone.

"Only when they deserve it," she answered quickly but lightly. Not quite a joke, not quite a put-down.

He laughed slightly, then after a short pause said, "I shouldn't have gotten mad."

"I'm sorry I pulled you through sh—" They spoke in unison.

"What?" she asked.

"I shouldn't have gotten mad," he repeated.

Sarah looked at him doubtfully. "Is that an apology?"

He gave a half-smile and shrugged. He watched as her eyes traveled the length of him, slowing near his thighs and then rising to his face again. Her cheeks were flushed when she looked back at the road.

He took another, closer look at her. He would have to be dead not to notice how attractive she was. Her dark hair was rich and thick. Her body was lean and sporty, yet still held the curves and lines of pure woman. She could rope, ride and drive, and her quick wit, while annoying, was also extraordinarily refreshing. It emboldened him to call her out. "What was that look for?" then enjoyed the way she shifted awkwardly.

She shrugged. "I'm happy you got a new shirt."

"Oh?"

"Well, I don't want manure on the seat." Her hand rubbed the faded and cracked leather. "I just had her detailed."

She glanced at Laine again, then back to the road. He could tell she was nervous, though he didn't know why. She had not been the least bit nervous while she was yelling at him. She drummed her fingers on the steering wheel and bit her lip again.

"I can't fire you, you know," he said. "It's been written into the contract with Letters End that the workers are to be retained."

"I know."

"If you know, then what's making you—"

"Are you going to pull funding for Starbuck?" Sarah blurted.

"What?"

"Starbuck," she said again. "If you're going to pull her then I need to know, because the Stampede is next week, and I will have to train—"

"Why would I pull funding?" His voice was even, the timbre of his words deep.

"Because I lassoed you and dragged you through cow shit. Because Starbuck is one of the most expensive animals at the ranch. Maybe you don't know how important the Calgary Stampede is. I yelled at you. Berated you. I don't know how to keep my mouth shut, and probably never will. And some people don't like that. Investors NEVER like that." She exhaled in a huff. She glared at the secondary highway.

Laine chuckled.

∾

SARAH HATED THAT HE LAUGHED. She had been stressing over this and he laughs?!

The masculine timbre of his voice unsettled Sarah; it vibrated down her core and had the hair on her arms standing on end. She looked at him again, uncertainty clouding her gaze. He was looking right at her, his eyes squinted, his smile cut a white path across his rugged face.

"Miss Steele," he said in a professional tone, "I would never pull funding for an action that was without a *doubt,* in my best interest. As for the yelling, well, I could do without that, but I would never ask you to censor yourself for my sake and wholly understand that if I am being yelled at, I probably deserve it."

The tightness in Sarah's shoulders relaxed. She believed him. His assurance allowed her to breathe again. "Well." Sarah glanced at him then back to the road. "I'm glad to see you have an ounce of good sense then."

"So, am I still an asshole?" he asked, a lightness was now in his voice.

Against her better judgment Sarah said honestly, "I don't know yet."

She was a little relieved when he chuckled this time. Maybe the champion bull rider had a leveler head than Sarah originally had given him credit for. She cast another glance at him as he cranked his window down.

The rolling hills with calves bounding through it and endless blue sky stretching into dusk did not distract her from the cowboy sitting next to her. Silence stretched, which was odd, Sarah didn't usually struggle with conversation.

"I don't really know what to say now," she confessed. He hadn't minded her honesty earlier. She figured she'd try it again.

"What do you mean?"

"I don't know." She shrugged, unsure how to put her feelings into words. She wanted to know what he planned to do, the changes he planned to make. Would she have to check with him or would she be allowed to continue making decisions? Would she have to report to Bruce as well as him?

"How will this," she said, waving her hand between them, "work?" She couldn't make out his expression, mostly because she could only catch quick glances of his face, but when he didn't say anything she clarified. "You're an investor. I'm a hand. Do I report to you?"

"What did you do with past investors?"

"Nothing really. They would come to the ranch occasionally. Check out how things worked, how things were going, then leave. They certainly were never at a roundup and absolutely never in my truck."

"Okay then." Laine nodded, his brows pushed together in thought. "Why don't you treat me like a new worker?"

"I would have fired you by now," she said quickly, then smiled so he knew she was joking, "so that doesn't bode well."

"Moving forward then. I'll try to stay employed."

Sarah nodded at that. Okay. She could get behind that. Moving forward.

"Oh shit," she exclaimed and looked behind her out the window.

"What?"

"I lost my hat." In all the commotion Sarah had forgotten it. The hat wasn't particularly nice, or fancy, but she'd worn the piece of felt for years.

"I gave it to Bruce. It blew off when you knocked the fence over."

"Oh. Thanks," Sarah muttered. It was nice of him to grab her hat. She cast another look at Laine. He took off his own hat, and ran his fingers through his slightly sweaty hair, ruffling it off his scalp. The red ring above his forehead gave a distinct line from the dust on his lower face to the white of his forehead. Sarah looked back out the window.

She rounded a curve, she knew these backroads that led to Letters End better than anyone. She took another corner and glanced at Laine. He didn't seem bothered by the speed she was driving. If Bruce were in the truck he would be holding the 'oh shit' handle by the window and yelling at her to slow down. Of course, if Bruce told her that, she would simply ignore him and continue to drive like she always did.

Her heart was still a little uneasy after being worried about Starbuck. If Laine had pulled funding, then who knew where the horse would go. Sold off to the highest bidder? Sarah's dreams of winning the coveted Calgary Stampede championship barrel racing buckle would be crushed, and all of her hard work training Starbuck would be for nothing. But he had told her the horse wouldn't be sold. And had assured her that even though she had yelled at him, her previous actions were okay, too. His assurances were very different from the wild bull rider she had heard him to be. His reputation was not very professional. But Sarah wasn't sure she could trust the gossip as truth. He hadn't shown much common sense earlier today; although he seemed more level-headed now. If he wanted to be civil moving forward, then she had to accept that. She hated the flutter of attraction she felt and didn't want it to cloud her judgment, so she tromped on the feelings, pushing them down, stashing them in a secret recess of her mind.

Nearing the turn to the Letters End Ranch, she pushed in the clutch, shifting the truck into a lower gear. The tires rumbled, edging closer to the shoulder.

The high gate that welcomed people to Letters End had been representing the ranch long before Sarah was born. Large wooden posts standing on either side of the huge gateway were joined by thick cross timbers vertically settled over top.

"I see that all over." Laine pointed to the log entryway as Sarah drove under it, her trailer bumping jerkily as it crossed over the cattle gate. He shook his head and raised his shoulders indicating his confusion.

Sarah's brow furrowed. "Where are you from?" she asked.

"Manitoba, why?"

"They don't have those," she said, jerking her thumb behind her, "in Manitoba?"

He shook his head. "Yeah, But I see them here more."

"Those posts symbolize a hitching post. A sign of welcome, a sanctuary for horse and rider."

"Really? I've never heard that before."

"My Nan told me that," she said, her voice quiet. "I don't actually know if it's true."

Sarah gazed at the green fields of Letters End Ranch, seeing a small cottage in the distance. A road over, it was tiny when compared to the vast prairie in front of them. No welcoming lights shone from the little house, and no smoke swirled out of the chimney. Her mind drifted back to the times she had driven home from the ranch, knowing a warm meal, cold beer and loving hug had waited for her there. The empty reality was so different from every single memory she had, that the pang of sorrow felt like a punch. "Nan knew lots of things like that. Had little anecdotes and advice for every little thing." Sadness must have shown on her face as they passed the little cabin.

"When did she die?" Laine asked. The quietly spoken question was laced with kindness.

Sarah heaved a sigh. "A little over five months ago."

"That sucks."

It was the understatement of the year and Sarah could not agree more.

"Yeah," she said, inhaling, "you know, Nan was a hand here her entire life. The stories she told would have knocked your hat off. She's the reason Letters End made it through the harsh winters when most ranches lost their herds. At least that's how she told it. She convinced them to lower the costs of running the ranch and keep as much as they could in-house. Which is why, to this day, Letters End still farms grains, unlike most cattle ranches and horse stables. The XYZ brand diversified, and that's what ensured its success all these years.

Do you see to the west, that bunch of trees over there?" Sarah pointed out her window. At Laine's nod she continued, "That's the west boundary. And ahead of us a couple clicks is the river," she explained, driving toward the stables.

The sprawling stables, barns and outbuildings of Letters End Ranch were picturesque in the setting sun. The large buildings were perfectly situated at the base of rolling hills and lush prairies. The white wooden fences ran the length of the fields, disappearing in the distance, and in the corner field the sprouting heads of wheat land crested as far as the eye could see. The golden colors brilliant despite the setting sun.

Sarah hauled the trailer down the well-worn gravel road that bent around the back of the stables. She knew every bump and jar and navigated them easily. She could hear Nigel getting restless in the back of the trailer, probably as ready to be done with the day as she was. Sarah pulled her trailer to the spot beside the barn where she always parked.

"Thanks for the ride," Laine said as he rolled up his window.

"Sure."

She waited when he did not get out right away. He was staring at her oddly. A sort of yearning in his expression, his body was relaxed and tight at the same time. He wanted to say something, but no words came out.

She guessed at what his concern was and said, "Nan always said if you're wanting to prove something... do it. Don't try and convince people you're capable. Action speaks louder than intent."

He pulled back and blinked at her. She must have hit it on the head.

"Moving forward, right?" he said, giving a half-hearted smile.

"Always." She jumped out of the truck, not smiling, but not frowning either.

CHAPTER 3

When Laine took off after closing the truck door, Sarah wasn't surprised. She probably would have, too. Hell, it had been an exhausting day and she wasn't the one who was yanked by a lasso and dragged for a bit.

"Hey Sarah, you want help?" Becca asked, opening the horse trailer.

"Do you want to help? Or do you want to gossip?" Sarah smiled at Becca and stepped into the trailer to unload Nigel.

"We can do both," Becca called after her.

Sarah guided Nigel out of the trailer; his hooves clopped along the metal floor then flicked a little when he got back onto solid ground. He shook his head and exhaled heavily. "I know, boy, we're almost done," Sarah said, comforting him.

"You lassoed someone!" Pam's high-pitched question almost had Sarah cringing. "I miss one day of the roundup and you freakin' lasso someone?!"

"You should have seen it, Pam," Becca said, soon grabbing the saddle from the trailer and following Sarah into the stables.

"Was he mad? I bet he was mad! I heard he's rich! Three-time champ! Kelly said he drives a lifted Dodge, and that he has the most incredible stallion." Pam talked excitedly, grabbing the saddle blanket and remaining tack from the trailer and pulling the door shut.

"Oh, he was mad! And I don't care that he's rich," Sarah answered. Her body ached, her eyes drooped from the long day and hard work. But she still followed the familiar steps of getting Nigel back into his stall. The smell of the stable was a familiar comforting scent; clean hay and dust. The dark wood of the stable could be seen for stall after endless stall. Almost all filled with horses. Different-colored manes and coats that stretched into the distance in the low light. Sarah lead Nigel to his stall. Her girl-friend followed.

"Pam…" Becca threw the saddle onto a stand in the tack room and bounded back out, "…you should have seen Sarah. So, this cowboy—"

"Laine Young," Pam added, the celebrity name vibrating off her lips.

"Right, Laine." Becca climbed onto the top rail of the stall. "So, after we got the cattle from the back forty, Sarah and I get to the staging area and—"

"I know, I know, Kelly told me." Pam waved her hands. "I want to know what he's like." Pam flicked her blonde, perfectly curled hair over her shoulder. "I mean, we all know what Laine Young stories are like. Remember, Claire said her cousin hooked up with him in Texas and he bought her new tack and then didn't call her."

"Oh yeah!" Becca exclaimed, "he was the one who Roman raced those pintos in Georgia and then had to buy them all because the owners were so mad."

Pam nodded. "Kelly said he was married like three times, then hid his money so the ex-wives couldn't get a cent."

"I heard he made money at the rodeo and then invested it and is now some super millionaire cowboy." She sighed and leaned on the post. "You drove back with him." She looked at Sarah. "What did you talk about?"

Two sets of eyes turned to look at her. "I don't know." She finished brushing Nigel.

Pam scoffed and looked to Becca. "Is he as cute as they say?"

Becca nodded seriously.

"Guys, we are grown women, don't we have something better to talk about than idle rumors or how cute some guy is?" Sarah asked.

"I know we're grown." Pam swayed her head to make her point. "And independent, and damn fine barrel racers, and we work hard for our money."

"Damn right," Becca chimed in.

"But I did all my chores," Pam stamped her foot, "and now I want some DE-ssert."

Sarah and Becca laughed.

Sarah asked, "So, you don't want to hear about the cattle roundup? Or the wild stallion? Or the wicked throw I did when I lassoed a man, saving him from possible death? No. You want to hear about his wide shoulders, and lean hips and how absolutely incredible his butt—"

"Sarah?" The masculine question from behind her had Sarah flipping around; her heart dropped, her eyes widened.

"Hi," she said weakly to Laine. Heat rushed to her face. He had walked down the dimly lit stable and was standing in the shadows, holding something black.

"He cleared his throat, a smile jerking at the corners of his mouth. "I brought you your hat." He offered her the worn felt hat.

She took the hat, smiling shyly. Not sure what he heard, not sure why she felt fluttering in her stomach, not sure what to say next.

"Thanks. We were just—"

"I know. I heard." He smiled. "I guess I'll see you later. Ladies." He tipped his hat at Becca and Pam. "I am going to walk away now." His cocky smile landed on Sarah last as he spun on his heel and sauntered back down the stable, fading into the shadows beyond.

"Definitely incredible," Pam whispered when he was out of earshot.

"That was nice of him," Becca offered.

"With a cherry on top!" Pam exclaimed.

Sarah bit her lip, staring down the dark stable not sure if it was excitement, embarrassment, or dread she was feeling.

CHAPTER 4

*E*arly the next morning, Sarah stood in the kitchen. The white sink basin boasted as many dents and dings as the island and long wood block countertops. Nan had loved the simple, clean and functional lines of the small but efficient kitchen. Sarah paused, tears welling in her eyes. She inhaled deeply, letting out the air in a controlled breath. Tossing and turning the night before, she had not slept well, unable to fall into a deep sleep like she usually did. She looked around the kitchen.

When Sarah was nine, Nan had finally relented and had purchased a modern range, but the woodstove still sat next to the 100-year-old hutch, which was filled with baking ingredients and cookbooks. Sarah pulled on the long-handled lever that held the ancient fridge door closed, then reached for the milk jug and poured herself a glass. She gulped down the milk, nuked a package of oatmeal, then spooned it into her mouth, standing near the sink. She had loads to do today, and eating didn't usually rate high on the list. She threw her dishes into the sink, grabbed her keys and rushed out the door.

The drive to Letters End was a five-minute drive. She hadn't wasted any time beginning the familiar list of morning chores. Her day had not begun well. It had taken her almost an hour to clean the horse trailer. Then when she was feeding the goats, she had slipped and dumped the feed onto the ground. Now, muddy goat hoofprints were tracked on her back.

When she left the coop after collecting eggs, the aggressive rooster took advantage of her distracted mind and bolted out the gate. Now he strutted around the yard like he owned the place, cockadoodling his annoying heart out.

Sarah had to train and work with the horses this afternoon, but she knew it would not go well if her head wasn't on straight. Nan always said the horses read a person's body language and energy. If her body language was distracted, then the horses would be distracted. Sarah gritted her teeth and dug deep for focus.

Whenever thoughts of the upcoming Stampede entered her mind, she shoveled faster. If she started to think about Nan's passing she would haul harder. If the image of that damn cowboy came into her mind she would spit and scrub with more vigor. She was in the feed barn when calm finally came over her. Sarah stopped hauling the heavy square bales of hay, breathing heavily. The pile she had stacked was impressive. She wiped the moisture off her forehead and took a moment to breathe in the dusty scent and look at the rays of sunlight filtering into the feed barn. She took a few deep breaths and enjoyed the moment of stillness. Her thoughts were quiet, there was no one around. Sarah was still. She headed to the large stable, ready to train some horses.

THE BLUE ROAN quarter horse was the most stubborn three-year-old Sarah had ever trained. The horse fought every command and constantly rebelled against her authority.

"Come on, Rouge, you know what to do." Sarah kept a tight grip on the reins as she kicked her heels into her mount's sides, keeping a tight squeeze with her knees. The horse sidestepped and stomped, but Sarah did not relent. "Go." She gritted her teeth, trying to aim the high-stepping horse towards the barrels placed in a triangle near the center of the large indoor arena.

It was a war of wills and a battle of stubbornness but Sarah knew she couldn't give an inch. She could feel the thin layer of sweat forming on her brow. Controlling the spirited mare took everything she had. Sarah's legs burned, her forearms stung, but she kept a tight hold. The horse shifted so Sarah squeezed tighter, pulling the reins again, stopping the rebellion before the stubborn horse could try to skitter sideways.

Rouge suddenly relented and tore across the dirt-packed stable towards the barrel at the other end. The horse's little but mighty legs carried her quickly to the other side of the arena, and with a tight pull on the reins, Sarah had the little mare twisted around the first barrel and streaking across to the second. The mare flew around the barrel, digging her hooves into the dirt and taking off. Sarah leaned into each turn, kicking her feet and saying encouraging words, all while gripping the horn and leaning over the pummel to get more speed out of Rouge. After the horse took the final barrel, she sped back across the arena to where they had started.

"Seventeen seconds!" Bruce yelled from the empty bleachers. "That was seventeen seconds!"

Sarah didn't take the time to smile or relent on the reins. She focused on guiding the spirited mare, maintaining control as she cantered to a trot and finally slowed to walk. Sarah directed the horse where to go, fully completing the training. Reinforcing what was expected. The beautifully colored mare huffed and slowed, finally giving her head and command to Sarah. There'd be a long road ahead with this young one, but the horse showed a lot of promise.

"Sarah, come here for a second," Bruce called to her once the horse had cooled down.

She swung her leg over the mare, her leather boots hit the

ground and Rouge shifted suddenly. Sarah reacted quickly, gripping the reins and pulling firmly on them.

"Whoa!" she soothed, when the horse pulled against the restraint. Sarah gave the horse a slap on the shoulder, not hard enough to hurt her, but sharp enough to let the large animal know that that behavior was not okay.

"Hey." Her sharp tone accompanied a firm yank on the bridle.

Bruce wanted to talk to her, but he would wait for her to deal with the horse. The spirit in the horse was unmistakable, but left unchecked she would become ornery and useless. Sarah gripped the saddle horn again and thrust her foot into the stirrup. She pulled herself into the saddle.

"Come on, girl, you can't act up like that and expect to get your way." Sarah pointed the horse towards the other end of the stable and kicked her into a full-out canter. The speedy mare ran the length of the arena for five minutes; until sweat formed on her underside and she heaved great gulps of air. Sarah again slowed her to a walk and allowed the girl to cool down.

This time when Sarah dismounted, the horse stood perfectly still, allowing Sarah to easily give the reins to a stable hand that came running over.

"Don't put her with Murphy, okay?" she told the young worker, "they fight. Put her next to Nigel, and don't give her any oats, they make her bloat. Only the feed from the green barrel next to Nigel's pen, please."

The worker nodded and walked Rouge back to the stables.

Sarah knew the horse would be taken care of. Brushed down and then let outside to enjoy the summer sun.

She headed to Bruce who was waiting in the empty stands that dominated one side of the large arena. Seeing Laine next to Bruce caused a little nervous tremor to flutter through her; but she didn't break stride as she went to talk to them.

"Hey," she said, slightly breathless. She flicked the hair out of her face then wiped the sweat off her forehead with her sleeve.

"How's she doing out there?" Bruce asked, his head nodding towards the now empty arena.

Sarah shrugged and rubbed her wrists gently, the dirt and sweat coming clean under her thumb. "She's stubborn. But we'll get there. She was left to pasture too long."

"Damn owners didn't know her true potential and left her on her own." Bruce nudged Laine in the arm, filling him in on the history of the horse.

"I found her up in—"

"Bruce," Sarah asked over Bruce's story. "What's up?" She interrupted him to avoid a long story about how people should or should not treat their horses, and Sarah did not have the time to listen to it... again. She wanted to get this over with as soon as possible and get out to check the fences.

It didn't help that Laine was standing there, on the other side of the wooden boards, looking fresh and clean and damn sexy. She did not want to get distracted by Laine, and didn't want him to look at her dirty, sweaty face, and flyaway hair, so she kept her eyes on Bruce.

"What are you up to today?" Bruce asked.

"I have to check the east paddock before that storm rolls in..." she trailed off, wanting him to take the hint.

"Great! I want you to show Laine around the property. If you are heading to the east paddock, that's perfect. Take Laine with you. Make sure to show him the feed storage, the big barn, and old red and the longhorns. If you go to the tack room, show him the ropes. Get it?" Bruce laughed at his own joke. He turned to Laine. "She knows this place better than anyone else. So, you're in good hands." Bruce clapped Laine on the back.

The thought of toting this guy around for the rest of the day put a stone in her belly. Wasn't the truck ride enough?

"Bruce, I can't show him all that in one day. Get Gary to take him."

"I don't want you to do it in one day, Sar, I want you to show Laine around for the next month."

Sarah couldn't help the scowl she directed at Laine. It was a mistake. First, because he made a face, reacting to her scowl, and second, because when she looked directly at him, letting his hazel eyes meet her stare, it was like the ground shifted. *Damn* he was handsome.

Laine stood silent as she glared at him.

"Let me know how the fence is out east," Bruce said, then strode out the side door of the arena.

"I saw your stallion earlier. Is he ready to ride?" she asked Laine.

Laine nodded. "If you're busy, I can get someone else to show me around."

Sarah weighed her options. She knew Pam was around here somewhere, or she could pawn him off on one of the stable hands. But she quickly dismissed the idea. Everyone was busy getting ready for the upcoming Stampede. She was heading out anyway.

"No. Come with me. Meet me in the main stable in a half hour."

THE LARGE GATE squeaked as Sarah pulled it open. Nigel followed easily, without a lead, slowly picking his sleek legs up and down, holding his head high. His glossy coat shone in the afternoon sun. He maneuvered his large body through the gate, circled easily and waited patiently for Sarah on the other side. Laine walked his horse through the gate onto the next paddock. The tan stallion he rode huffed out a breath and gave his body a shake, his feet sidestepped as Laine urged him through the gate.

"Heeey," Sarah warned in a low voice; the unfamiliar horse was eyeing Nigel. The tan horse huffed once more but stopped shaking his head.

"I haven't broken him in yet," Laine apologized. He pulled hard on the reins to keep the horse from bolting.

Sarah pulled the large gate closed, pulling the wire hoop that secured the top post into place. She moved to Nigel, who was waiting patiently for her. She scooped up the reins, wrapped her hand around the horn of the saddle and grabbed the back cantle with the other. Once she swung her leg over his large rump she settled into the well-worn saddle, finding the stirrup on the other side without looking.

"Ready?" She clicked at Nigel gently encouraging him, and he trotted off briskly without waiting for Laine to answer.

Nigel trotted over the pasture of green grass, but Sarah knew he wanted to run. She kicked up the pace, giving Nigel his head and the older horse leaped into a canter, his long legs carrying him over the field easily. Sarah held the reins in one hand and rested her other hand on her thigh. The position was familiar to her, and comfortable. Her body relaxed into the melodic rhythm of her horse. The air in the afternoon held a warm sweet scent. The buzz of grasshoppers a constant hum in the background. The sun, hanging in the sky without a single cloud to blemish the endless blue, beat down on the prairies casting the green grassland into a dreamy light. Sarah loved this time of day. The grass seemed a little greener, her horse ran a little smoother, and her heart beat a little faster.

Laine matched her speed on his gorgeous stallion. His horse yanked and chomped on the bit; Laine constantly pulled on the reins trying to stop the stallion from getting out of control. Sarah leaned back in her saddle, Nigel slowed at the command. Laine's stallion gained on Nigel, pulling into the lead.

Sarah didn't mind, a smile snuck onto her lips as her gaze tracked Laine. His butt bounced and lifted in the saddle, keeping the gait of his horse. She enjoyed the rounded firm view for a moment, a gentle tingle spread through her body as she watched him. She ground her teeth but did not look away. His thighs hugged the pristine new saddle. His back was broad, she hated that she liked that. His hips narrowed from his strong shoulders, and now she was looking at his butt again.

Sarah shook her head and forced herself to distract her attention away from the cowboy.

~

"THAT'S A BEAUTIFUL HORSE. Arabian? Maybe Hungarian, Andalusian?"

Sarah's words startled Laine. "He is." He didn't add anything else, her knowledge impressed him. He normally would have been proud of his new tack but her old worn gear called to something deep inside him. Longing nagged in his core; for that history, for that devotion, for that pride.

Noting Laine's distraction, his stallion shifted, forcing him to fight to regain control. He could ride a wild bull, but this expensively trained stallion was giving Laine a run for his money.

The stallion sidestepped and slowed to a canter, veering closer to Sarah's horse. His long legs skittered awkwardly. Laine tried to pull on the reins but the stubborn horse pulled his head and tried to take a nip at Nigel.

"Hiya!" Sarah yelled, commanding her horse, who dug in and sped up. The riders tore across the field. Sarah leaned low in the saddle, standing in the stirrups and squeezing her thighs tightly.

Damn. She looked incredible flying across the field. Her worn jeans cradled her backside as she bounced in the saddle, posting gracefully to the rhythm of the horse. Sweat pooled between her shoulder blades, dampening the back of her sleeveless tank top. Her arms were fit and tanned. The muscles defined from working with horses every day. Her jeans were dirty and as worn as her leather belt. Hell, her whole outfit was worn, from her boots to her felt hat. In spite of the dirt and grime, she was stunning.

Pushing the distracting thoughts aside, he urged the stallion to catch up.

~

SARAH SLOWED Nigel when they neared the river's edge. Both horses were breathing heavily, sweat glistened on their bellies and ribs.

Thick grasses gave way to ice-cold waters and a slow-meandering river. Silver willows and large cottonwoods cast shadows over the water. The shade was blessedly cool.

Sarah hopped off Nigel and watched as Laine yanked the reins to slow the stallion. She knew the young stallion probably had not run often so was out of shape. His heavy breathing and foaming at the sides of his mouth, confirmed her suspicion.

"Hop off." She cocked her head to Laine.

"Why'd you go so fast? If your idea of a tour is seeing the pasture in a green blur, then well done."

The stallion shook his head and pulled at his reins.

"I want to try something." Sarah readjusted her hat, securing it after the swift ride, getting ready to face the stallion.

Laine glared at her from his tall horse. His brows almost touching, his gaze staring down his masculine nose at her was highlighted by a sheen of sweat glistening on his brow as he tried to still the stallion.

"This isn't a tour," she said firmly. "I'm not your guide. Get off your horse or learn to control it." Her terse tone resonated over the panting of the horse.

The stallion balked, side-stepping. Laine reached for the horn and pulled on the reins.

"Whoa," Sarah cooed to the stallion. She grabbed the bridle on his chinstrap to stop him from bolting. His large dark eyes blinked at her, he huffed out his breath, not from exhaustion but stress. "It's okay, honey," she spoke to him, "you're okay." The horse stilled. "Shh," Sarah soothed. She looked up at Laine. "Get off."

He scowled down at her. Sarah didn't look away. The confrontation turned into a staring contest, her versus him. A battle of wills. His unbreaking stare told her he didn't like being told what to do, but neither did Sarah.

She waited.

"Fine." Laine shook his head and swung his leg over to dismount.

His tall body passed uncomfortably close to hers. She ignored him and gave her full attention to the horse.

She reached up to grab the reins, pulling the two unconnected straps of leather into one hand. "Hold this." She gave Laine the reins. "But not tightly." She stroked the incredibly soft coat of the horse. "What's his name?"

"Caspian Rutledge Carmack, the third."

Sarah stepped closer to the stallion's head and petted his thick neck. "Hello, sweet Cas, you're a good boy."

She ran her hands along his neck, and down his shoulders. "There you go, honey," she said, her voice even and reassuring. Her hands traced the large muscles along his chest and down his legs. The horse huffed, still breathing heavily, but the quivering in his legs began to slow. "It's okay, you're okay," she repeated.

Sarah continued stroking the horse along his back and flank for a few more minutes. She didn't think about Laine, or Nigel, or the Stampede or the cloverleaf of barrel racing. She focused on her hands, how they traced the horse's curves, and on her voice, making sure it was calming, and on her own energy, centering herself and standing a little straighter and lowering her shoulders a little more. Her fingers followed his muscles and pushed gently when she felt a knot, smoothing over it firmly. She pushed with the palm of her hand down his flanks then turned back to his head and face.

She pulled on the bridle snap and readjusted it around the horse's eyes. "There you go, sweet thing," she whispered to him, stroking along his shoulder to the cinch that wrapped around the barrel of the horse's chest. She put her fingers under the new cinch and pulled, feeling the tension there. She slipped around the horse and pulled at the latigo. The belt-like piece loosened in her hands, relaxing a notch. She ran her hands under the blanket that protected the horse's back from the saddle and tugged on it, shifting the whole thing off his withers. She then pulled the cinch tight once more.

Cas let out a sigh. Standing completely still, his eyes half-closed as Sarah came around the back of him, letting her hands tell him where she was the whole time, talking to him in quiet tones until she came full circle to his face once more. She stood next to Laine but ignored him as she finished. Her hands smoothed down the hair on Cas's gorgeous face; she patted him once more on his cheek and rested her head on his forehead.

The motion knocked off her hat, but she stayed like that, enjoying the connection, and the relaxing moment.

"What did you do?" Laine asked in a whisper.

"What do you mean?" she asked, not moving from the horse.

"Well, look at him." Laine lifted the reins that hung limp between his fingers. The tan beauty was standing calmly, not shifting his feet, just standing. Waiting. His ears shifted slightly, he breathed evenly.

"His tack is new and needed adjusting. It will get worn in eventually, but until then you should make a habit to adjust it, so it doesn't rub." She felt him looking at her closely. "My nan would have said it's easier to break in a new man than it is to get tack right." She smiled at the memory. "Here," she said, motioning for him to stand beside her as she shifted to the side of the horse. "Do you feel the muscle here?" She grabbed his hand and guided it under her own to show him what she was talking about. Laine stood close to her. She could smell the fresh scent of detergent on his clothing, but she stayed focused on what she was saying. "Do you feel that knot?" She pushed gently with her fingers. "He aches just like we do. Massaging them out is useful. The run helped, too. He was made to run, look at him," she said, leaning back, "he's gorgeous. But with a breed like this, they can turn wild and untrainable if not treated right."

"I can't believe that worked so fast." His expression echoed his disbelief.

"Yeah. It's relaxing. It's a massage." She shrugged.

"I didn't think you could give a spa treatment to a horse."

Sarah laughed. "Well, it's not a spa treatment. But he works his muscles like the rest of us. Don't you like your muscles massaged?"

Laine shook his head. "Can't say."

"You've never had a massage?" The skepticism was etched into the turn of her eyebrows.

"No. I don't see the point."

Sarah shook her head. "You've never had one, so you don't know if you like or need one, but you're telling me that you don't see the point?" She put her hands on her hips.

Laine raised his shoulders.

"Here," Sarah said, stepping closer to Laine, "give me your hand."

Skepticism etched his brow, but he offered her his hand. She reached out and put both her smaller hands under his and gently placed her thumbs on his palm. She was suddenly intensely aware of him and regretted her impulsive action but did not pull away. She used pressure to push along the palm of his hand, following the muscles. She shifted her pinky fingers to lace through his fingers and bent the hand slightly, allowing full access to his palm and wrist.

Sarah felt his hand relax beneath her touch. She glanced at his face, his expression unreadable at first but then his features relaxed and a small smile tipped his lips.

"That feels…," his quiet voice trailed off.

"And that's just your hand, imagine if I worked a bigger muscle." She meant it honestly, meaning the bigger muscles on the horse, but the widening of his eyes made her realize her mistake in word choice. "Like on a horse." She stumbled out. She dropped his hand and rubbed the big stallion's thick shoulder muscle instead.

Sarah shifted, Laine did not. She was trapped between the horse and the cowboy.

"Anyone can do it." She tried to continue the conversation, while looking everywhere but directly at him. His closeness was off-putting, causing butterflies to flitter in her stomach. When he didn't move, her eyes darted to his face.

His gaze took in every feature of her face. She would have looked away if there was anywhere else to look, or if her face would listen to her brain. But all she could do was look back at him, her mouth getting drier. She wanted to lick her lips, but even her tongue was not working. "It's easy really..." She tried to keep talking. And when he didn't say anything, her uncomfortable emotions evolved quickly into agitation and she asked sharply, "What!?"

His expression altered immediately, his eyes widening and his shoulders squaring. "Nothing."

The stallion lowered his head and nudged Sarah a little.

"It's time to go," Sarah said, handing Laine the reins.

She whistled a sing-song tune and Nigel trotted out of the water and directly towards her.

Cas stood straight, his ears pointed towards Nigel, his shoulders squared and proud. Sarah gave him a gentle nudge, and a lowly spoken, "Hey." The intelligent animal broke his stare with the approaching stallion and lowered his shoulders.

She held Nigel's reins onto the horn and hefted herself into the saddle. The cold water from the river soaked her horse and shocked her calves.

She waited for Laine to mount. Cas stood quietly as he did so, and she headed Nigel along the river to the east paddock.

They ambled along the edge of the river, clean ice-cold water on one side, and lush fields on the other. Sarah wished she could just take in the scenery. But the final notice of her utility bill was on her mind. The vet bills were due. And she needed a new water heater.

She felt Laine's eyes on her. She looked behind her, and there he was. Watching her. She frowned and faced front again.

Before she headed to the Stampede grounds next week she would have to make sure the stables were clean, and there was enough feed for the goats, and she would have to check with her neighbor, Ashley, to see if she would feed her animals.

She looked behind her. He was staring at her again. She scoffed and nudged Nigel into a slightly faster walk.

If she asked the bank if she could pay for the vet bills on a credit line, then…why was he looking at her so much? Shouldn't he know it's rude to stare at someone like that, for that long.

She twisted in her saddle. Maybe she was just imagining his eyes boring into her.

Nope. He was a few paces behind her, and he was not contemplating the scenery, the breathtaking mountain view, or the river valley and stunning countryside. His slightly furrowed brow stared unnervingly, right at her.

~

LAINE HAD TO GET A GRIP. Riding in the gorgeous prairies should have been a pleasure. But riding behind Sarah was distracting, not to mention his damn horse kept trying to dance sideways. He had promised himself he would be different in Alberta. He wanted to be a better man. He knew there were crazy rumors about him, and that most of them were not true… not entirely true. He did have an energetic past when it came to women, but he liked to think he was also a pretty decent guy.

His ex-wife probably had a different opinion of him, but didn't all women have poor opinions' of their exes?

From the first moment he had heard about Sarah Steele, and then seeing how she behaved at the roundup and the stables, he had an undeniable admiration for her. When she walked through the stables the workers would pick up their pace and stand taller. She gave praise easily and never chastised without good reason. When she worked with horses there was a smooth grace between animal and human. He had worked with many amazing women at the rodeo. But none had captured his attention like Sarah. She was stunning to be sure, but there was something else about her that had him staring at her, embarrassingly so. He was caught between trying to figure her out, and just being in awe of her. Her strength, confidence and talent were undeniable.

He watched her, wanting to take every opportunity to learn from her. He found it slightly off-putting that she obviously wanted nothing to do with him. He ignored the deep attraction just as fiercely as he ignored a need more primal than logical. He convinced himself that he could learn from her and get to know her without making the mistake of sleeping with her. He was sure of it. But the way she was looking at him, or more like glaring at him, he was obviously pissing her off. He shook himself mentally. Maybe he should stop looking at her and get to know her.

"So, how many years have you been working here?"

RELIEF JUMPED through Sarah when Laine finally broke the silence and rode abreast of her instead of slightly behind her. She didn't understand his earlier brooding looks and welcomed the cordial tone he suddenly had.

"My whole life," she answered. "I was raised not far from Letters End. Just a little farther east. We passed Nan's house when we came back yesterday," she said, pointing behind her, away from the towering Rocky Mountains. "I guess it's my house now." Her comment didn't feel real. The house wasn't hers, it felt like she was just staying there until Nan came back. If only Nan could be there, at the kitchen table, with a coffee and a good ear when Sarah got home. Sarah shrugged, despite the pain. "My parents split when I was a kid. Nan pretty much raised me. No," Sarah corrected herself, "not 'pretty much', she absolutely raised me."

Laine rode quietly next to her. His body rocked with the easy stride of his stallion. His cowboy hat was low on his face and his hands gently held the reins resting on the saddle horn. He was perfectly handsome, and if she counted right now, he was perfectly amicable.

"Do you see them?" he asked, turning his gaze to catch her looking at him.

"What?"

"Your parents. Do you see them often?"

"I haven't seen my mother in years, and my dad's a trucker. So he isn't home that often. He was in Dallas when Nan died, and he couldn't make it back for the funeral."

"What did you do?"

"Do you see your folks often?" She cut off his apparent interview with a question of her own. Why was he asking her so many questions?

"Umm." He blinked. "My mother and step-father are still in Manitoba. I see them whenever I can."

"And I heard you were married." She tried to sound pleasant.

He paused. "Yup."

"Not anymore?"

"Nope."

Sarah understood he didn't want to talk about it. She couldn't blame him. Who wanted to talk about failed relationships? She sure didn't. She changed the subject. "You seem tall for a bull rider."

"That's probably why I wasn't any good at it."

Was he trying to be ironic or humble? She gave him her unimpressed look. His misplaced modesty could take a hike.

They rode across the prairie to the far east paddock. The lumbering herd of longhorn cattle were dark spots in the distance.

Sarah inspected the fence as they went, making mental notes of the loose sections that would require repair.

They continued along the river's edge. "The red barn is over there," Sarah said, pointing as they crested the riverbank and came onto the prairie again. "Bruce stores the combine and tractors in there over the winter. And that," she said, pointing to an old red barn, with an arched roof and large double doors, "is one of the original barns. It still has the antique batteries from when the farm was government-owned and had its own power, one of the first in Alberta."

"This place is absolutely gorgeous."

Sarah nodded, it was one of her favorite places on the ranch, too. "Yeah. There have been lots of people looking to buy this quarter and tear down the barn to build a fancy house or hotel."

"Yeah, I know."

Sarah's eyes shot to Laine.

"I have been approached to sell it." Sarah's face must have shown her appall. Laine quickly added, "of course I wouldn't sell it. Look at this place."

Sarah smiled. "I couldn't agree more."

"Just before I moved out here my best friend from high school died. Heart attack. Just like that." He snapped his fingers. "Dead. He was my age." Laine looked at Sarah. "It just really shakes you, you know. I really looked at my life and had to make some hard choices. So, I came out here and I guess—wholly shit! Are those Percheron?!" His excited change in attitude and sudden alert posture made Sarah smile.

They had ridden past the barns to the next white-fenced paddock. The sprawling green hills were speckled with large horses. They stopped by the sturdy fence to look into the next pasture.

"Yeah," she said though it was unnecessary. Laine's attention was completely taken away by the herd in the connecting pasture.

She smiled, understanding his reaction. Large horses dotting the green field were enormous and held a certain majesty. Their thick shoulders, broad faces and coloring made them stand out like an artist's rendering of a Western dream with the back drop of the snow-tipped Rocky Mountains in the distance and rolling green fields in the forefront. The horses were mostly gray with dark speckles of black and white. A few were a lustrous dark brown, their coats glistening in the afternoon sun. And many had white socks at differing lengths up their legs, or black socks drifting up their thighs. They lifted their enormous heads, their widely spaced eyes tracking the approaching horses and riders.

Nigel whinnied a greeting, Cas took a few steps sideways, and a few Percheron whinnied back. Laine stood in the saddle, lifting his hand to block the sun. He twisted to look at her, a question in his glossy eyes.

She inhaled and pursed her lips and whistled. Loud. The melodious sound was sharp and made Laine duck oddly, bringing his shoulders to his ears. But it was worth it when an answering whinny caught Laine's attention and he jerked back around. The herd that had been scattered in the field responded to the familiar sound with excited cries and sprang to movement.

Sarah quickly hopped off Nigel. Laine followed her lead and jumped off his stallion. She took the reins from Laine's hand and tied Cas to a post farther from the wooden fence penning in the Percheron. Nigel would be fine with the herd, but she was unsure about Caspian. She flicked off her hat and hung it off the saddle horn then went back to the fence, whistling again softly.

The enormous horses ran towards the humans in a seemingly practiced synchronized movement, all gathering in a thunderous wave and clamoring over the green fields.

Laine stood close to the fence and watched. Sarah could not see his face, but his posture was rigid as he stared at the herd of Percheron barreling towards them.

The gray and white draft horses threw their heads as they closed the distance to the fence in a loud heaving, massive muscled wave to finally come to a stop by the fence. Huffing and stomping they came to an abrupt halt, their breath coming in excited heaves.

"Holy crap." Laine took off his hat, still marveling at the impressive stock.

Sarah smiled and walked to the fence; she reached her hand out to the largest in the herd, cooing gently to him, "Hello, kitten." She stroked the large head leaning out over the fence. The horse accepted her touch with a slight quiver to his haunches. She pet the towering horse gently along his cheek and down his wide face.

"Kitten?" Laine walked slowly to stand next to Sarah.

She shrugged. "I didn't know he was going to be this big," she said, patting his cheek, "but he was always this sweet." She laughed when Kitten nudged her shoulder and nestled his head close to her; she brushed his cheek again, and he stilled, enjoying the caress.

The wind whipped her hair slightly, and the fresh smell of summer grasses and afternoon sun blew over the prairie. The snow-capped mountains in the distance were glistening a brilliant blue and gray.

Sarah loved these moments. Her arms lifted to fully wrap around the horse, loving the way he leaned into her, with his solid frame, so large yet so gentle. His lips curiously nibbled her arm, the soft motion comforting her, making her smile slightly. A few more Percherons reached over the fence to greet her. She patted each large head and cheek, getting lost interacting with the gentle giants. Knowing them since birth, having ridden and trained them, created a bond Sarah would never take for granted. She laughed gently as Sampson nudged his brother out of the way to reach the tall grass outside the fence. She cooed gently as she brushed hair out of Fancy's face. Kitten's large head pushed against her again, and she leaned into him, hugging his huge head.

～

LAINE HAD BEEN MESMERIZED by the enormous horses, but it

was Sarah who captivated his attention now. She stood in the midst of the great heads, a soft smile on her lips as she patted and spoke gently to the horses. Her unabashed abandon held him in awe. She was so competent and confident. He felt something tug inside him, something he had never felt before. His attraction to her was there like always, but this was something different. He *wanted*. He *yearned*. It was unnerving, and uncomfortable, and he couldn't do anything about it but continue to watch Sarah interact with the horses.

CHAPTER 5

Sarah stared at the stoic cowboy, uncomfortable with how long she had stood there, wondering if she had said anything stupid while talking to the horses. Nope, she was good. But the expression on his face reminded her of earlier when all he could do was stare at her.

He was watching her now. His entire body still. An odd expression on his face. She couldn't read it. His dark hair was blowing slightly in the wind, and his eyes held such depth Sarah almost looked away, but she couldn't. She didn't look away. She stood there, staring at him, with Kitten's large dark head draped over her shoulder.

"Do you want to pet him?" She wasn't sure if the wind took her words or if she truly sounded slightly breathless.

Laine didn't look away as he stepped closer, closing the gap between them. Butterflies fluttered in her stomach as he approached, his gaze never leaving hers. A few Percheron leaned their heads farther over the fence, sniffing the stranger. But Laine's interest was not piqued by the horses.

He stopped in front of her; she had to look up to maintain eye contact. She raised her chin. She took a breath. Her nipples hardened at his nearness, and when his large hand reached out and gripped her upper arm gently, excitement drove through her.

The impulse to wrap her arms around his tall shoulders flittered through her mind. She wanted to push herself against him, crushing her body against his hard one. His lips were full for a man, his eyelashes long and dark, and his facial hair held a day's growth of beard. And though his eyes were dark, they seemed lit with something bright and exciting. He reached out with his free hand and brushed a dark tendril of hair away from her forehead, his fingers taking their time as they stroked the fly-away strand behind her ear. He didn't lower his hand but allowed it to rest, cupping her cheek.

"This is going to be a problem." He shook his head regretfully as he slowly bent to kiss her.

Sarah's heart raced. Her body cried out to be touched by this handsome cowboy. If his hand had not been on her arm, she probably would have thrown herself at him already. He was so close to her, her body tingled with excitement, her toes curled in her boots when she—

What did he say?

It took Sarah a moment before she registered what Laine had actually said.

Her a problem?

Her hand flew to his face, catching his chin and squishing both cheeks together in a tight grip. His lips pursed awkwardly from the pressure and his eyes rounded with shock. She would have laughed at his expression if her heart wasn't pounding and anger hadn't flared inside her.

A million thoughts flew through her head. All her responsibilities, the pressure of the Stampede, final notice statements, Letters End... what the hell was she doing standing here in the field with this guy. She had been ignoring the feeling brewing inside her all day, and then she had let her guard down. Which had been a mistake.

She pushed his face back and took a step away to gain some distance.

"Don't!" She glared at him when it looked like he was going to follow her. Nigel stood straighter, alert to her tone. "Just… don't."

She was mad. She had let Laine distract her so that she had forgotten to keep him at arm's length. His genuine interest in the ranch had been welcome, she always loved talking about it. But then he was there, and she was there, and he was so damn sexy and even his damn brooding behavior was attractive; though she hated to admit that. There was a draw to him that went deeper than his devastating smile.

But she had seen this happen before. Women getting involved with their bosses. Or getting involved with bull riders. Or getting involved with Laine Young. And it never ended well. Sarah had lost too much this past year. She would not make Letters End, her last sanctuary, become a place she wanted to avoid. Not because of one cowboy. Nan would say: *don't shovel shit forward.*

"Sarah." He seemed to struggle for words. "I didn't…"

"I don't want to hear it." She just wanted to get out of here. "You tried to *kiss me*. Don't blame me for your lack of self-control. I am not the problem."

Sarah called to Nigel and the horse trotted closer. She swung into the saddle and without saying a word or looking back, moved Nigel into a canter and tore away. The herd of Percheron may have watched her leave, but she only felt one man and his penetrating stare, boring into her back.

CHAPTER 6

Two days had passed since Sarah had shown Laine around the ranch and grabbed his face and yelled at him. She wasn't avoiding him exactly. Though she wasn't going out of her way to see him either.

When she and Becca had been training in the big arena, she had felt Laine watching her from the sidelines. She pretended he wasn't there and kept herself busy with various tasks. She really did have to check on Rouge on the other side of the stables. And when Bruce had called them all in for a lunchtime break, Sarah's truck really did need air in the tires. She had better things to do than socialize with Laine.

Okay, she was avoiding him.

Sarah shoveled fresh hay into the stall she had just cleaned. Sweat dripped off her temples and slid down her back.

"There you are! You disappeared after running barrels this morning." Pam swung into the empty stall. "Are you trying to break records at mucking as well as rookie of the year at the Stampede?"

Sarah was out of breath. "No. I just want to get caught up." She continued to shovel in fresh hay.

"The hands can do this," Pam said unnecessarily.

Sarah knew the hired stable hands could muck out a stall. But she was doing it. Agitation fluttered in her chest.

"Laine was asking about you," Pam said, trying to gain Sarah's attention.

"Yeah." Sarah didn't stop her energetic shoveling.

"He had all kinds of questions about how you train, and what you do here, and—"

Sarah stood and swiped her hand across her forehead, pushing the wisps of hair off her face. Her chest rising and falling in agitation, she looked at Pam. "So?"

"So... I'd wanna know if he were talking about me. I thought you'd want to know, too."

Sarah shook her head and bent to finish her task. She jabbed the pitchfork into the fresh straw and she shook it out in a dusty sweet-smelling carpet.

"You're gunna have to see him sometime," Pam said seriously, "and he really isn't all that bad."

Sarah gave her a not impressed look and continued spreading the straw.

"Bruce said he ordered a new tractor. And I heard he was looking at putting extra insulation in the arena so it's not so cold in there. And Kelly said Laine was gunna sponsor anyone who wanted to compete next year in the High River rodeo."

"That's great, Pam. Really. But that doesn't make him a great guy, it makes him a rich guy, and all those changes will directly affect his pocketbook at the end of the day."

"He gave Becca the larger stall in the main stables for the same cost she was already paying," Pam said.

"Well, that's nice." She relented, turning her back on her friend to get the straw into the far corner.

Pam didn't take the hint. "I talked to him earlier. He seems really nice. I showed him Spitzee and Spitzee took to him, and you know what a good judge of character she is."

"That horse would be nice to a cactus, Pam." Sarah stood.

The straw was evenly laid out, there was nothing left for her to do. "And I'm not avoiding him. I have lots to do, and don't have time to deal with him. And the house and preparing for the Stampede." Sarah inhaled shakily. "It's just a lot, you know. Nan would have been here to help me through it all."

"I know." Sympathy laced Pam's words and softened her eyes. "I thought the distraction would be good for you." She shrugged. "I just want to make sure you're okay."

Tears pricked at the edges of Sarah's eyes. Sorrow had a way of sneaking up on a person. "It's been months." Sarah chewed on her lip. "I thought it would get easier."

Pam closed the gap between them and wrapped her long arms around her friend.

"I'm okay." Sarah lied as tears gathered.

"Nan would have loved seeing you at the Stampede." Pam leaned back to look at Sarah. "I know she was proud of you." The kind words made Sarah smile.

"She'd tell me to stiffen up my lip and quit crying in the straw." Sarah looked around at where they stood. "Literally."

"Yeah. But then she'd make you cinnamon buns and drink whiskey with you all night until you felt better."

Sarah nodded and blinked a few times. "Yeah," was all she was able to say. She took a breath. "Nan won her first Stampede in trick riding and barrel racing."

Sarah walked out of the stall with Pam keeping step beside her. "She told me it was never about the win, but about the thrill of the ride." They turned to walk down the empty stalls. "I just wish she could have seen me at the Stampede."

"I know, sweetie." Pam draped her arm around Sarah's shoulders as they walked, her taller frame fitting a few inches over Sarah's. "Life ain't fair sometimes." She paused, then said, "But I think we are pretty good at finding the joy in it."

"Thanks, Pam." Sarah hugged her friend. Her heart ached for

her Nan, but Sarah was so thankful for true friends, she almost started to cry again.

Pam rubbed her back. "Anytime, sweetie."

They smiled at one another, then Pam said, "Be nice to the strange cowboy so the strange cowboy can be nice to you!" She winked and sauntered off, veering toward the other side of the stables. Sarah rolled her eyes then started off to the main arena. She had some training to do, so grabbed a bucket and headed to the water trough out back.

Sarah strode through the barn to the other side where the large doors were wide open. The sun was a welcome sight from the dim light in the stable and the dust from her morning chores. She had almost made it out of the shadow and into the light but stopped dead in her tracks, her empty bucket swinging.

Her purpose was forgotten, her breathing non-existent and her conscious thoughts went mute.

Laine was standing in the late morning sun in nothing but boots and blue jeans. His wide shoulders and lean torso were completely bare and were they sparkling?

Sarah blinked.

He *was* sparkling. Her muddled brain sluggishly put together that he was standing by the water trough, so he must have rinsed himself off.

Her assumption was confirmed when he shook his head like a dog shaking its butt, shooting droplets around him. The spikey damp hair a dark halo around his head. He bent to reach into the water barrel and pulled out his shirt. He twisted the dripping fabric, squishing water from it. Sarah swallowed and watched his arm muscles contract to wring out the shirt. The muscles on his stomach rippled slightly, highlighting the gentle six-pack there. Her gaze traveled over his amazing body and then drifted lower where a light spattering of dark hair narrowed to disappear below his belt.

There was something incredibly appealing about a guy in

nothing but jeans and boots. She swallowed, and continued to stare at him, hidden by the shadows in the barn.

Laine gripped his shirt in a fist, and rolled his shoulder a few times, as if working out a kink. He did the same with the other one, letting his muscular body flex in the sunlight. He raised his arms and stretched his back, leaning back, flexing this way and that. His twisted torso highlighted his muscles and he moved his shoulders and flexed the rounded defined muscles there as well. He let out a low moan.

Sarah wasn't sure if it was pleasure or satisfaction that she heard in his sigh, but her body responded like he was speaking right to her feminine bits. A shiver ran down her spine, despite the summer day, and she inhaled unevenly. The tingle in her womanhood and tightening of her nipples made her squirm.

Laine's attention shifted. He turned to look directly at her, his gaze landing squarely on her face. The shadow, apparently, had not hidden her as well as she had thought.

"What's with you?" she asked, regretting that her tone was aggressive. Embarrassed to be caught, she just kept staring. Did he know how long she had stood there? Was he doing all that flexing on purpose? Could he see her hard nipples through her thin shirt?

"I was helping Bruce fix that back fence and I got hot. Why were you staring at me so long?" His eyes widened, and he gave her a pointed look.

"So your shoulders are sore from actually working today?" She ignored his look and his damn question and asked her own.

"Someone lassoed me a few days ago. I think a little bruised shoulder is expected. Why were you staring at me so long?" he asked again, this time a smile pulled at his lips.

Arrogant man.

Sarah scoffed and turned to walk back into the barn.

"Don't you need water?" Laine called, "or do you just carry that around with you for fun?"

She could hear the teasing in his tone. Sarah gritted her teeth, not a hundred percent sure why she was agitated and why she wanted to smile at his behavior. She equally wanted to slap him. Couldn't the man leave well enough alone? Hell, couldn't the man just leave?

Sarah turned slowly and walked from the shadows of the barn into the warm sunlight. "Are you gunna put your damn shirt on?" she asked as she dropped the bucket and turned the hose that was next to the trough on to fill it up.

"Why?" He looked at her gleefully. "Does it bother you?"

The bucket filled quickly, and Sarah slammed the tap back off. "No, it doesn't bother me. But your back is burning, and I don't want to hear you complain about a sunburn as well as your allegedly bruised shoulders." She yanked up the bucket and made her way around the back of the barn trying to make a quick exit. But Laine had other plans in mind.

"Where ya going?" He jogged after her, pushing his arms into the sleeveless shirt and putting on his black cowboy hat.

Sarah stopped and put down the bucket, turning to face him. His shirt was on, but the button up was still very wet and hung open, revealing his amazing body that tempted her to gaze at it again. She glared at him instead.

"All covered up." He patted his shoulder. "No burn here today."

"Laine, what do you want?" Sarah asked. Her tone was a mix between impatience and curiosity.

"I want to know where you're going," he said simply.

"I'm doing chores. I just cleaned out the chicken coop, fed the pigs, bottle-fed three calves, mucked out the stalls and am now heading to train with Starbuck."

"With a bucket of water?"

"Yes. The water is for wiping her down. It's hot, we sweat, she chafes under the cinch, so I give her a wipe down afterwards." She stared at him expectantly. "Any other questions?"

"Can I come with you?" The playfulness was back in his eyes.

"You own the place." She swung around to swipe up the bucket and strode towards the arena, ignoring the contradicting bubble of excitement and irritation that flittered through her as he followed behind her.

"I don't *own* the place." Laine kept stride with her.

Sarah raised her eyebrows doubtfully. "Do you own a large share of the corporation that invests in Letters End?"

He hesitated before answering. "Yes," he said, drawing out the answer.

"Are you able to make decisions as they relate to the financial condition of Letters End?"

Another hesitant, "yes."

Sarah stopped and turned to look at him. "Then let's not split hairs. Investor, corporate sponsor, owner," she said, shrugging her shoulders. "What's the difference?"

She turned and walked briskly toward the stalls again.

"I can't fire anyone I want. Even if I'd like to."

Sarah understood he was joking, the way he jogged beside her and his intonation made that clear. Which is why she barked a laugh. "Ha! There *is* some justice in the world."

SHE VEERED into the stables and dropped the bucket outside the stall that held Starbuck.

"Hello, my sweet girl," Sarah called to the dark chocolate brown horse who greeted her with a shake of her head and a gentle exhale of breath. Her tail flicked, and her ears were forward. Starbuck nestled her head against Sarah accepting the gentle petting. The happy nickers that came from the horse clearly exclaimed her excitement.

Laine stepped closer and Starbuck lifted her head, her eyes focused intently on the strange man. A bang from inside the stall rattled the wooden boards. Starbuck kicked backwards again, another bang. Sarah opened the stall door and pushed the horse firmly back. She kept her hand on Starbuck's shoulder, her touch firm. "Hey now." She kept her voice low.

The horse's ears perked again, her eyes looked at Laine. There was no more kicking of the barn walls.

"Come closer, but don't raise your hands."

"She doesn't seem to like me." Laine didn't move.

"It's just because you were next to me, and we are in her space. Come closer."

Laine took a tentative step towards the stall.

"Closer," Sarah encouraged.

Laine stepped within a foot of the stall. Sarah made a wispy sort of noise and said, "Off." Starbuck moved quickly. Her long neck reaching, her teeth bared. Laine closed his eyes and ducked his head. His hat was nipped off and flicked to the side, coming to a dusty skid next to one of the barn cats. The cat watched the hat skid past him, and sauntered closer to Starbuck's stall.

Sarah smiled as Laine muttered, "Jesus," under his breath, and then bent to get his hat.

Sarah bent to Starbuck's rear leg to wrap tape around her ankles. When she stood up Laine was standing at the stall door looking in. Starbuck was happily sniffing the cowboy, and the barn cat was in Laine's arms, eagerly getting scratches, little cat feet kneading the air in feline bliss.

The image struck Sarah in an odd way, pulling at a feeling of yearning. Sarah quickly bent to wrap Starbuck's front ankles.

She stood to get the saddle but Laine was already there with the saddle blanket and heavy saddle. It surprised Sarah. "Thanks," she said as she placed the blanket and then hefted the saddle on.

Laine heard her surprised tone. "I am more than just a pretty-faced bull rider, you know."

Sarah wanted to scoff at that, but instead looked directly at him and with a level tone said, "Are you?"

His equally direct gaze held her hostage as she watched the play of emotions flicker over his features. "I want to be."

The blatant honestly was uncomfortable. Sarah tore her eyes back to the saddle and pulled the cinch and straps in place.

Once the sleek and beautiful horse was ready, Sarah led her out of the stall.

"Ready?" She met the horse's eyes.

"Sure," Laine replied.

"I was talking to the horse," she said, leading Starbuck to the doors.

The outdoor area was smaller than the indoor one. Which made sense considering the outdoor arena was only used for half the year and was buried under snow for the other half. Sarah preferred the outdoor dirt-floored area over the inside. Who wouldn't. The Rocky Mountains as her backdrop, the sun shining down on her, and a horse to work with. She couldn't ask for anything more.

Laine stayed on the outside while Sarah led Starbuck into the fenced corral.

She walked to the middle of the corral knowing that Starbuck would follow obediently. She held the halter loosely, speaking in soft tones to the horse. The little Appaloosa had the sweetest temperament and was a delight to work with. Her very dark brown coat and white mane made a stark contrast. She had no white markings on her feet, but there was an intricate-looking starburst on her muscular chest that was echoed on her rump; the white pattern looked like paint had been thrown at the shiny horse. Sarah felt Laine's eyes on her, which made butterflies contort in her belly. Did he know how much the horse cost? She could never dream to own such an expensive horse; Letters End held that honor alone. But Sarah had trained the young mare with impeccable bloodlines since she was a two-year-old colt, so she had invested more time than anyone could count.

She glanced at Laine. She didn't like that he was just standing there. His long arms were crossed and resting on the top of the fence. His hat casting a shadow over his eyes. She hated that she could not see his face. He still looked gut-catching sexy cast in shadow and light, and skin and jeans.

Starbuck side-stepped, unsure what Sarah wanted her to do. Sarah shook herself mentally; she had to focus. She stroked Starbuck's lustrous forehead and began putting her through her paces, clipping a long tether to start warming her up.

She clicked Starbuck to a run, warming her up in a circle. Sarah was very aware of Laine. His quiet staring was the most annoying thing at the moment. And there was nothing she could do. She couldn't yell at him or chide him or tell him he was annoying her. He was here. And there was nothing she could do about it. She had never dealt with something like this before. Things were changing and she didn't like it.

An image of his dripping torso and chiseled smile flashed in her mind. Starbuck dipped her head.

"I know, Starbuck," Sarah whispered to the horse, "he is annoying me, too." The lie did not make her feel better. The horse was sensing Sarah's distraction. Starbuck couldn't care less about the audience.

"Hey, Sweetheart!" Bruce called as he walked around the corral.

Thank god!

"Morning," she called back not bothering to stop her training, but the smile that spread across her face was genuine.

She heard Bruce chatting with Laine, and the burning feeling in the back of her neck lessened and she was able to focus wholly on her barrel horse.

Laine was doing nothing that a million other people had not done already; he watched her work with horses. She had to get her shit together. Sarah took a steadying breath and focused.

She slowed Starbuck to a breathy walk and brought the horse closer to her. She took off the long tether. Sarah moved her hands gently, clearly telling the horse what she wanted her to do. The velvet mare bent her knee like she was taught to, allowing Sarah to mount easily, slipping her cowboy boot into the stirrup and gliding onto Starbuck's back. She clicked gently again, and the horse moved to a walk and slowly into a gentle trot to continue warming up.

"She looks good, eh?" Sarah heard Bruce say to Laine.

"Unreal," Laine answered. Sarah had no idea what he meant by that, but she glared at him for the comment, and ignored the ping of flattery she felt inside. She pushed Starbuck into a quicker trot.

"She barrel races, too, smooth as glass, that one. Can corner a barrel on a dime." Bruce snapped his fingers.

The comment from Bruce made Sarah smile. He complimented her often, but only when she had truly earned it, and while she had heard him gush about her to other people, she found particular satisfaction that Bruce was telling Laine about her skill now. She kicked up the speed a little and started guiding Starbuck towards one of the barrels in the arena.

"I heard," was Laine's response.

"They said there is no other like her. She's pretty rare," Bruce continued.

Sarah wanted to scoff. No other like her? That was laying it on a little thick even from Bruce.

"Is that so?" Laine asked. His tone seemed genuine, which was weird to Sarah. She would have thought he would be sarcastic, or snide. What was with that?

"And," Bruce continued, "her bloodlines are impeccable."

This was getting weird. Sarah's brow furrowed.

"I really like," Laine said next, "the chest area—"

"Hey!" Sarah yelled, trotting Starbuck over to the men and breaking her warm up routine but figuring enough was enough. "I am *right here*!" She was appalled that they would speak like that about her, like she wasn't even there.

Both men had equally shocked looks on their faces. Did they think she couldn't hear them? Did they think she would be okay being spoken about like she was a piece of livestock?

Laine burst out laughing. "You thought we were talking about you?" he said between laughs, then started chuckling again.

Embarrassed heat spread across her face; she felt it rise from her chest, neck, cheeks and forehead.

Bruce tried to stifle his laugh, but a little burst came out.

"That's what you thought, isn't it?" Laine asked again, but at her blank expression he laughed again.

"Sweetie," Bruce said with a smile, "we were talking about Starbuck."

Sarah glared at them. Which seemed to make Laine laugh harder, and the smile on Bruce's face widened.

"You better be talking about her," Sarah said. "But you forgot to mention she can do this!" Sarah yanked on Starbuck's reins and spun her around and bellowed an excited, "Heway!" The mare's legs dug into the dirt and she sprang forward.

Sarah leaned over the horn and kept her arms tight beside her, aiming Starbuck to the first barrel, off to the right side. When the pair got there, Sarah pulled and kicked at the same time. The horse knew the command and knew what was expected. Her rear legs closed the gap to her front legs as she skirted the barrel in a blink. And then tore across the dirt field to the other barrel. Sarah's heels encouraged the horse to run and run she did. Careening around the second barrel, Sarah hung onto the horn as the little mare flew around it and headed to the final barrel in the cloverleaf pattern.

Starbuck practically leaped around the final barrel, turning perfectly when Sarah cued her to do so and barreled, ears back, legs reaching, returning to where the men stood.

She slowed Starbuck, letting her walk off the sprint.

Sarah cast a glance at the men. Bruce had a proud smile stretched across his face. Satisfaction and excitement crinkled his brows.

Laine must have pulled back his hat during her ride because she could clearly see the shock and awe written on his features.

It gave a satisfied sort of tingle through her core.

"Wow," she heard Laine say under his breath.

She smiled despite herself, and patted Starbuck on the neck. "Good girl. Good girl."

"Well done." Laine clapped and gave a hoot. "I've never seen anything like that, Sarah. Wow."

Pride blossomed through her. She hated that she loved it, but impressing Laine felt good. She hadn't felt at the top of her game lately, and with Laine watching her all the time she felt a little exposed.

Sarah trotted around the ring, enjoying the warm sun, and thinking maybe Laine wasn't such a bad guy after all.

CHAPTER 7

*T*he knock on the door startled Sarah, not because she was covered in flour, sweating in the middle of her kitchen, but because anyone she knew, knew not to knock. The door was never locked. She tried to keep the irritation from her voice when she hollered, "Come in." The door opened, and a pair of boots trod into the house. "I'm in the kitchen!" she called again as she pushed the sticky dough across the big wooden island.

Laine appeared in the large doorway that separated the kitchen from the living room. His hat was off, leaving his dark thick hair slightly squished to his head and a little red mark along the front of his forehead.

His dark brown eyes gave nothing away as he took in the scene in the kitchen.

Sarah knew she was a messy baker. The pile of bowls, measuring cups and spoons overfilling the sink was nothing compared to the chaotic scattering of ingredients on the counters that surrounded her.

She didn't stop kneading the dough, though she would have loved to wipe the sweat from her forehead or maybe pulled back the tendrils of her hair that had escaped her loose bun. But the dough waits for no woman, and her ego would have to take second place to the buns.

"Bruce said you might need some help," Laine offered. He fingered the buttons on the cuff of his long sleeve plaid shirt and rolled up his sleeves.

The pull of attraction when he rolled up his sleeves almost distracted her. The small movement of rolling up one's sleeves had never occurred to her to be sexy, but on Laine… she pushed the dough harder on the counter.

"Really? Yeah, I'd love some help. Can you grab that glass pan," she said, pointing, wiping her sweaty forehead, "and wipe butter around the edges…" her nose pointed to the pink butter dish "… and then bring it to me?" She cocked her head once more and slapped the dough onto the island.

Laine grabbed the glass dish and paper towel to spread the butter inside. "Man, is it hot in here."

"Wood stove." Sarah nodded to the corner where the cast iron wood stove sat in the corner like a fat baker. "Nan didn't like to get rid of things. We usually use the new stove," Sarah said, motioning to the modern white gas stove resting near where Laine was leaning on the counter, "but honestly, food, especially buns, tastes so much better in the wood oven."

"That's what you're making? Buns?"

"Yeah. Cinnamon and dinner." Sarah stopped to wipe her forehead with the top of her forearm. "I am on the last batch. Then it will be too hot to do anything in here."

Laine's gaze roamed over the mess in the small but spacious kitchen, using a piece of paper towel to push butter into the glass pan. "How long have you been at this?"

"I don't know, three hours? I wanted to get them done yesterday, but…" she shrugged. She blushed thinking about the erotic thoughts which had kept her up all night. She barely made it out of bed in time to feed the chickens, let alone make buns.

"Here." Laine stood in front of her with a generously greased glass pan.

Sarah blinked at him, wondering if he could read her thoughts. She didn't look in his eyes.

"Thanks." She took the pan and put it on the island. "Can you put on those mitts," she asked, pointing with her white powered hand, "and take out the cinnamon buns from the oven? Just be careful, it's hot."

Laine did as he was asked and strode to the large black oven. Sarah inhaled when he opened the door, the sweet smell of cooked, slightly browned sugar and butter filled the kitchen.

"Just put them on the sill there, please," she instructed him, pointing with her eyes to the windowsill. She beat the large dough ball she was working with a few more times. "If you want to roll these buns with me, that would be awesome."

The sentence made Laine laugh. "Sure, I'll roll buns with you." He walked to the sink and washed his hands.

She rolled out the dough into a log and used the back of a knife to divide up the dough into small palm-sized balls. She then took the soft, smooth dough and held it in her fist. "Put the dough gently in your fist, like this." She showed Laine. "And then use your other hand to push the dough through your finger and thumbs, like this." She pushed the dough through and then tucked the tail ends under the smooth surfaced ball and placed it on the greased pan.

She watched as Laine grabbed a dough ball and mimicked her. His large masculine fingers pushed gently to form the bun into shape.

"Like that?" He held the ball up.

"Yup, perfect." She hated that her voice sounded dry. She cleared her throat. "They have to rise for about half an hour and then they go in the oven for about twenty minutes."

"Why do you need so many buns?"

"Oh, it's for the Community Center fundraiser. Just a little thing we do before the Stampede. People who live nearby, or work at Letters End get together and raise money for different charities. Nan and I were always in charge of the buns…" her words trailed off. "I didn't even think about it. I just figured I'd make them this year, too."

She felt her brow crinkle, and a hollow sadness swirled in her belly. She'd heard people say that it would get easier with time, but the ache was still there.

Laine picked up another ball of dough and pushed it through his fingers, the second one going faster than the first.

"You're a natural." Sarah smiled gently at him.

Sarah cast glances at Laine as she formed the buns. He didn't seem to be a bad guy. As she got to know him, he seemed less arrogant. Or his arrogance was there but he was not acting on it. Thinking of what Pam said about accepting Laine, she guessed she could give him a chance. She looked at him again, and a nervous flutter hit her gut. Sarah took a breath. Nan would have clucked her tongue at her behavior. *Be a straight shooter, sweetie*, she could almost hear her Nan say.

"How are you liking it here so far?" Sarah tried for a pleasant tone.

Laine patted the ball of dough gently and placed another one into the pan. "It's gorgeous. Everything. The mountains, the prairies, the river. The ranch is incredibly well run, and," he said, pausing to look at Sarah, "I'm liking it."

She smiled. "Good." The pan was full of perfectly rounded buns. Sarah put clean tea towels over them. "There. Now we wait."

Laine picked up the sticky bowls and sugar bags.

"No, no, just leave it. I have to sit for a second and get out of this heat."

Sarah washed her hands and dried them. While Laine was washing his hands, she stepped to the side table with the pile of bills with bold red OVERDUE notices on them and the large intimidating manila envelope from a lawyer's office she refused to open and hid them behind the microwave.

She smiled at him when he turned and headed into the living room.

The double doors that led out to the wrap around deck were open, letting in the sweet cool morning air. The room was filled with cooling cinnamon buns and the dinner buns Sarah had made that morning.

Laine wandered over to a pan with rolled sugar and cinnamon buns almost spilling over the top and inhaled. "They smell delicious."

"If you want one, just—"

"I want one." Laine smiled, a boyish twinkle in his eye.

Sarah smiled, too, and went to the kitchen. She came back with a knife, two plates and two cups of coffee.

"Nan never needed a recipe. Just knew how to do it from scratch." She cut out two soft cinnamon buns. "I don't know how she did it. I wrote down what she did when I was younger, and I have made them more times than I can count. But I always have to read how much sugar, and how much flour to put in. I wish I could bake like her."

She plopped down on the couch, enjoying the relaxing pleasure of sitting after standing for so many hours. The creamy buttery sugar and cream cheese had melted into the fresh-baked roll. She took a bite, enjoying the heat and fresh taste of Nan's recipe.

Laine ripped the moist bun open; steam rose from it emitting a mouth-watering fragrance in the air. He took a large bite. He smiled with his mouth full, his tongue slid out and ran along the corner of his lips. Laine moaned with pleasure.

"These…" he shook the bun in his hand, not putting words to the pleasure on his face.

Sarah stared at him. Then realized she was staring at him and snapped herself mentally. She shoved more of her cinnamon bun into her mouth and, nodded. "Mmm hmmm. Nan always had a way with baked goods," she said around the food in her mouth.

She watched Laine study the sparse living room as he chewed.

The house had not been updated since Sarah could remember. The three-bedroom house had a small living room, kitchen and one bathroom. It reflected an antique store more than a modern household. The log walls were decorated with pictures and tack. The couch Sarah was sitting on was as old as her grandfather. The large stone fireplace was handcrafted with stone from the river bank.

"The bathroom has updated plumbing, and the kitchen of course. But there is still the original pump out back," Sarah answered before he asked.

He nodded, looking at the log ceiling, his eyes coming to roam over the pictures and ornaments on the fireplace.

The mantle held a smattering of black and white pictures, of her Nan, and the ranch, and the Stampede. Pictures of Sarah riding Kitten; her graduation, her first barrel race. There were a few trophies from when she was kid, 4-H ribbons and a bronze sculpture of a herd of horses.

Laine paused at the end of the large wood mantle where a colored picture of Nan sat next to a framed poem. For some reason Sarah held her breath. She watched his masculine back as he reached for the frame. Holding it in his hands, he began to read:

> You gently touched my leg and said,
> "I'm not afraid to die."
> You told me you knew that I was strong,
> and that I shouldn't cry.
> And then you kindly told me,
> as tears rolled down my face,
> That all you truly hoped for,
> was to pass away with grace.
> And you worried that when you were gone,
> I wouldn't feel you near,
> That when my heart was breaking,
> I wouldn't know that you could hear.
> But I know that you'll be there for me,

like you have been all these years,
All the times that you have held my hand,
and helped me fight my fears.
I know that you are with me, each and every day,
And I'll remember what you told me,
what your heart was trying to say…

You said:

Please don't cry for me, for I am never truly gone.
My arms may no longer hug you,
but my love is still so strong.
I'm with you for coffee in the morning,
and will kiss you before you sleep,
I am cheering all your triumphs,
I'll give you strength for when you weep.
I will always love you, I will always be near,
When you speak to me in quiet times,
I promise I will hear.
I will always love you, I know that you love me.
I will never leave you, so please don't cry for me.

Sarah listened to the quiet cadence of Laine's voice. The timbre followed the beat to the poem perfectly and it tugged at her emotions.

"That was for Nan," she said. "It was read at her funeral. We scattered her ashes over the fields and some down by the river." Sarah cocked her head. "She has been dead for five months, and I swear I still come into the house expecting to see her drinking coffee in the kitchen."

"How'd she die?" Laine's voice was quiet. Reverent. He sat next to her on the worn patterned couch.

Sarah took a breath before answering. "Cancer." Sarah

shrugged. "She didn't tell me when she was diagnosed. Not until she couldn't hide it anymore, then it happened pretty fast."

Sarah grabbed a photo from the table beside her and handed it to Laine.

She watched his expression as he studied the photo. Her grandmother and her as a preteen, smiling a toothy grin, standing like a super hero next to a 4-H cow with matching blue ribbons.

"You look like her," he said.

Sarah laughed and took the photo back. "I've heard that before. But she," Sarah said, shaking her head. "She was a titan. Nothing stood in her way." She looked at the familiar photo, at the woman who raised her, who encouraged her and who left a gaping hole now that she was gone.

"You know," Sarah said, reaching to put the photo back on the side table, "she was winning awards at the Stampede when women had just barely got the right to vote. Can you imagine?" She smiled. "Women were only *just* allowed to vote, and there my grandmother was, breaking records and being awarded more money than some of the cowboys won." Sarah barked a laugh. "I bet it pissed off a few of 'em!"

"Sounds like she loved every second of it."

She shook her head. "She was a force, you know." She nodded, thinking back to all the things her Nan had done. "She built this house."

"Really?"

Sarah stood up and crossed the living room to grab an old bound book from the shelf. She sat next to Laine with it. The worn leather had faded different colors and it had a few stains on it, and in the front stamped into the cover in uneven block letters was the word: Memories.

Sarah opened the book, flipping through the worn pages. The familiar scent of dust, and ink and memories had her tucking her feet under and snuggling deeper into the old sofa, her thigh close to Laine's. He rested his arm along the back of the couch and leaned in to look. The yellowed and browning photos reflecting historic Western life, sat securely on the aged pages.

She flipped through until she found what she was looking for.

"There." She pressed open the book to a photo of the cabin. The black and white glossy print had uneven edges but was surprisingly clear.

"That's my grandfather and that," she said, pointing to the skinny woman smiling broadly at the camera, "is my grandmother."

She smiled at Laine.

"That's one of the first Percheron she bred and broke." Sarah pointed to the awkwardly shaped photo below the one of the cabin. The white-spotted horse stood sideways, the girth of the beast easy to see. A thin young woman standing next to him held his halter loosely. Her head only came halfway up the horse's chest. Both horse and Nan were looking at the camera.

Longing stirred in Sarah. Her grandmother had been such an incredible woman. "She had worked hard on the farm before the men went to war. While they were gone, she worked twice as hard to make sure the farm survived and had bred the Percheron for military use. She had managed to raise three children, work a full-time job at the ranch, keep her own little farm afloat and still be a three-time barrel race champion.

"Nan didn't talk about it much, but I don't think my grandfather was much help. I heard more stories of him drinking than helping much after the war."

"At least he came back," Laine offered.

Sarah shrugged, not sure if that was true or not. Sarah was still paying off the debt of mistakes her grandfather, long dead, had left as her inheritance. Her Nan had made the most of everything though, not complaining. Just doing what she could to survive and raise her young granddaughter.

Sarah missed her so much, loved her so much it hurt, and wished she were here to tell her it was all going to be okay.

She turned the page, blinking the moisture from her eyes. The next page held one of Sarah's favorite photos. It was her grand-mother in her Stampede Western wear. Her leather riding skirt was a weird sort of baggy but did nothing to take away from her thin waist, tall frame and long arms. Her tight black curly hair was the same color as hers. The smile on her grandmother's face was victo-rious and unrepentant as she held the large championship belt buckle in front of her. Pearl Steele was a champion.

Sarah looked at Laine. "Sorry, this must be boring to you." She closed the scrap book.

"Not at all." He shook his head and opened the album back up. "I never knew my grandparents. My folks split when I was young, and my grandparents lived far away or passed away before I got to know them. The way you talk about your Nan is," he said with a shrug, "something."

"Better to have loved and lost and all that?"

"Maybe." Laine shrugged. He looked at the photo album again and nodded towards the next picture. "That's a great picture."

Sarah didn't look at the photo but kept staring at Laine. There was something still and attentive about this usually arrogant cowboy. It was comfortable sitting here with him, in her modest living room, in the middle of cooling baked goods with her dusty old photo album. He seemed genuine and curious, a side she hadn't seen before.

He pointed to another black and white picture. But instead of being crisp and clean this one was blurred, yet oddly beautiful. The herd of Percheron had been captured running through a field. Their bodies close together, their manes trailing gloriously behind them. The large individual heads of the beautiful horses could be seen clearly, but their legs blurred together, tugging, creating a feeling of freedom.

"It's one of my favorites." Sarah smiled knowing Nan had taken the picture. "You know, Letters End made a name for itself by supplying workhorses during the First World War. And in fact, most Percheron lineage can be traced back to a few corporate ranches in Alberta. Nan always wanted the Percheron to regain the recognition they once held. The prestige. And I guess they are, in some ways; they still cost a fortune, and are pretty desired. But these horses helped to win the war, you know. I can't wait to see them in the spotlight. Stampede is having a Heavy Horse show this year, so they will be showcased there, which is awesome. But—"

Sarah stopped talking. She was about to apologize for rambling, but when she looked at Laine there was a serious expression on his face. He was watching her intently and the look in his eye made a wave of cool tingles run through her body.

Breathless seconds passed.

The microwave timer beeped.

A sad yearning swept through Sarah as the timer broke the moment they were sharing.

They looked at each other and stood, shaking off the connection.

"Let's get the last of the buns in the oven and the kitchen cleaned. The fundraiser is tonight and I have a heck of a lot to do between now and then."

"Sounds like a plan." Laine led the way into the kitchen.

In the back of Sarah's mind, she knew she would call Becca. For some reason, she wanted to look her best tonight. She smiled, looking forward to it.

CHAPTER 8

*A*fter cleaning the house with Laine and finishing chores at the ranch, Sarah went to Becca's house to get ready and now regretted the decision as Becca threw clothes options at her.

She pulled a tank top over her head. "You sure you don't mind me wearing it? I might get a hole in it or something." Sarah adjusted the blue and black top, so it sat properly over her belt.

"Sarah, you look amazing." Becca shook her head as she said it. "Why can't my clothes fit me the way they fit you?"

"Your clothes fit you just fine." Sarah playfully waved her hand over Becca's dramatic show of cleavage.

"Well, I never!" Becca's horrible Western accent made Sarah laugh.

Sarah was satisfied with her efforts as she turned back and forth in front of the mirror. The jeans she was wearing were too tight for working at Letters End. They hugged her hips and made her bum fill the jeans in an attractive, rounded mass. She wore her only pair of nonwork boots. The intricately etched dark brown matched the scrawl on her belt. Her borrowed tank top was decorated with faded splashes of blue, black and pink that was feminine without being girly. Its decorative hemline fell in uneven lengths to her hips.

Becca came at her with a palette of blushes and brushes. "I am capable of putting on my own make-up, Becca," Sarah said.

"Yes, and you do a wonderful job of it. But this occasion calls for more definition, this time we have a purpose." With that statement, determination gripped her friend and an hour later Sarah had creams and lacquers on her face and had parts of her hair straightened, parts curled and all sorts of gels and spays put in and every strand tugged and pulled.

"You know I usually just wear a hat," Sarah had groused after a particularly hard pull at the hair at the nape of her neck.

"Pain is beauty," Becca sing-songed.

"Whoever came up with that saying should be shot." Sarah cringed as more hair was pulled.

"Whoever came up with that saying knew how good you could look with a little blood and tears." Becca smiled. "Go take a look." She nodded toward her bedroom mirror.

Sarah couldn't help but smile. She did look good. Her black hair fell down in waves, and for the first time in her life, controlled locks. The look was both wild and sophisticated. And even though it felt like Becca had put more make-up on than a hooker or clown would, Sarah's face was evenly defined, her features shaded and highlighted to stand out.

"Thank you, Becca." Sarah smiled at her friend.

Becca stood behind her friend and they looked at the image in the mirror.

"You have always been beautiful." She kissed Sarah on the cheek. "I just made a few minor adjustments." Becca let go of Sarah and backed out towards the door. "I invited Laine and told him you would give him a ride home at the end of the night." Becca squealed as she darted out of the room, a pillow close behind her. "Don't mess your hair," she yelled at Sarah.

~

SARAH DIDN'T ALLOW herself to break stride as she jumped out of the truck and slammed the door. She beelined it for the heavy barn door type front entrance and strode into the Community Center. She was uncomfortable with how much effort she had put into her look. She usually just yanked on jeans and a plaid shirt and threw a hat on. Why had she gone to so much effort? She paused and took a calming breath.

The Community Center was part bar, part hall. It was filled with her neighbors, and friends, and people who worked at or utilized Letters End. She saw Pam standing in a group of her friends.

"Wow girl, you look good!" Pam smiled brilliantly at Sarah.

"Thanks. Becca did it." Sarah shrugged and ordered a beer.

"I would like to welcome you all to this event." Bruce stood on the small stage awkwardly holding a microphone. "I see a lot of familiar faces, but some new faces, too. I want to personally welcome each and every one of you to the twelfth annual community charity event." Bruce waited for the applause to subside.

"The charity this year is, as most of you know, the Veterans Alzheimer's foundation. One hundred percent of tonight's donations and proceeds will go to the charity, so drink up, eat up, make your bids on the silent auction and be sure you have a good time." He stepped down from the stage, signaling for the festivities to begin.

A bit of a warmth, an awareness touched Sarah's outer senses before it registered in her mind. Someone was watching her. She turned.

Laine was sitting with a bunch of the people from the retirement home. The group of old-timers were sitting at one of the many large round tables and were laughing. Their semi-toothless smiles gaped a jagged line, but the merriment and mirth in each jiggling shoulder was clear.

Laine was looking at her. Staring directly at her, and Sarah could clearly feel the heat of his stare. A tingling sensation coursed through her, pooling in her loins and increasing her heart rate.

How could one man, with one look, do that to her? She was paralyzed, unable to move from his stare. The crowd surrounding her dimmed. The noise inside the Community Center faded.

"Oh my god, who is that?" Dianne whispered to Sarah. The comment jarred her, knocking Sarah out of her trance.

"That's Laine Young," Becca offered. Sarah was startled that she hadn't seen Becca come in or hear her join their circle.

"Oh my god!" Dianne whispered again. "He is staring at you so hard, Sarah. You should go talk to him."

The comment made Sarah roll her eyes. "Dianne, if he wanted to speak to me he would come over"

"Oh my God!" Dianne whispered. "He is coming over here." The last word came out close to a squeal.

Becca clapped her hands and said excitedly, "Hook line and—"

"Hello, ladies, can I buy you all a drink?"

"Yup," Becca answered happily.

"Bud all around?" he asked the group of women and flagged down a server.

Sarah watched him interact with her friends. They were full of questions and he answered them all easily. They asked about the stables, and where he was from, and his rodeoing. She sipped her beer and listened to them moon over him. Rolling her eyes from time to time. Dianne put her hand on Laine's arm, thanking him for the round of beer. He moved slightly to dislodge the contact, but said, "You're welcome," with a smile.

Realization that Laine was actually trying diligently to change, hit Sarah pretty hard. Nan's words came to Sarah, *a horse can't be broke, until he chooses to break.* All the rumors and gossip about him may have been true. But if Sarah was honest, he had been a stand-up guy since the day after they met. He had been cordial and kind, and generous.

He chatted easily with the people at the Community Center. Smiling and shaking hands with members of the community.

"He's not Trevor, you know," Pam whispered honestly to Sarah, as they both watched Laine.

The comment took Sarah off guard. She knew he was not her ex-boyfriend. The lying cheating man could rot for all Sarah cared. She had only been dating Trevor for a while, but when her Nan died he took off, never to call again.

"I know," Sarah defended.

"Then why do you have that look on your face?" Pam asked kindly.

Sarah wasn't sure what expression she wore. "I don't know."

"Sarah," Pam said, using a firmer tone, "you are the person I go to for advice and you have never failed me. You are worried, and stressed, and I can't imagine everything you are going through. I don't know what to tell you right now." Pam sighed. "If you were me and I was feeling how you are feeling right now, and everything that has happened to you had happened to me, what advice would you give me?"

Sarah looked at her friend oddly. *What?* She wanted to give herself advice? What would that even look like? Events from her life ran through Sarah's head. Her mother leaving, her father being away, her Nan dying... and suddenly something clicked. "I would say that people who you have trusted deeply have left you. But that doesn't mean everyone will leave you. That doesn't mean to never trust again."

Pam smiled. "Great advice, Sarah." Pam lifted her beer bottle and saluted Sarah with a smile.

Laine caught her gaze from across the group and nodded towards the dartboard.

Sarah shrugged. "Sure." She kept in mind the advice she had just given. She didn't think of herself as a jaded person, but deep down perhaps she did have trust issues. The hurt of her loved ones leaving cut deep, but that did not mean those wounds couldn't heal. That did not mean she shouldn't try to be friends with Laine.

They broke away from the group and made their way to the far wall where a dartboard was hanging.

"Careful, you don't want to poke your eye out," Sarah said, handing Laine three darts from the board.

In answer, he looked pointedly at Sarah, took one dart in his hand and tossed it at the board. The solid thud confirmed he had hit the horsehair target, the heavy dart jutting out of the green circle just outside the bullseye. "I think I'm okay," he said smugly.

Sarah snatched up a dart, shifted to face the board and pitched it. She didn't even try to stop the cocky smile that erupted on her face as her dart hit true, right in the middle of the circle.

"I guess I'm the one who poked an eye out. A bullseye." She laughed at the corny joke, and regretted it a little, but was rewarded with a smile from Laine.

He laughed, his eyes twinkled with it. "Oh, you wanna play? Let's play."

Sarah smiled ruefully. "Yeah! But you can't wear your hat."

The comment took Laine back a moment. His face contorted slightly, and head pulled back. "Why not?"

"'Cuz your hat distracts me, and I want to see your face." Her hand waved over him, motioning to the whole of him, though they were only talking about his hat.

It took him a moment to respond, but then he lifted his hand and took the black hat off his head. He placed it on the table as he ran his other hand through his thick locks to loosen them.

Sarah knew she couldn't take the comment back. What was she thinking asking him to take off the hat? It was foolish to admit she wanted to see his face, but she skipped over the weird feeling the confession gave her as she gazed at him. Now she could see his expression. No shadow obstructed his contoured cheekbones, thick perfect eyebrows and dark stubble. His nose was wide, but perfectly symmetrical and his eyes were an amazing deep brown. There was something appealing about this cowboy.

Earlier, he'd been attractive helping her bake, but tonight... tonight he had a raw sexual attractiveness that just kept drawing her in.

Shit, how long had she been staring at him? "Th-thanks."

His eyes narrowed. "If I can't wear my hat, then you have to wear my jacket." He pulled his jean jacket off.

The comment took Sarah back a moment, her face contorted slightly, and her head pulled back and tipped to the right. "Why?"

"Because this," his hands waved like hers had over her body, "distracts me. And I want to see your face." He was mocking her, but the look in his eyes sent an incredible thrill up her spine.

Sarah wasn't sure when it had happened. Or how it had happened without her approval. But she was flirting with Laine. And it felt right.

"Fine," she said, doing him the same courtesy of not belaboring the embarrassing request with looking too deep into its meaning. She snatched the jacket from his hands and thrust her arms into the warm sleeves.

"And don't use the coat as an excuse if I beat you," Laine said, pointing to the baggy waist and loose chest of the too large coat.

"Oh, I won't," Sarah said as she did up the gold-colored buttons. She enjoyed the masculine smell on the jacket. Of hay, and barn and whatever men put on to smell so good after they shaved and—

"It's called aftershave."

Sarah looked up at Laine. Did she say that out loud? She smiled. "I won't need an excuse, as I am going to kick your ass."

He laughed, perhaps mocking her slightly, but Sarah accepted it. He strode to the dartboard and pulled out the darts.

"Diddle for the middle?" he said, playing with the plastic flights on the back of his darts.

"Diddle for the middle," she agreed and positioned herself to toss the first dart.

They played 'round the world'. The goal was to hit all the numbers from 1 to 20 around the dartboard and then hit the bullseye in the middle.

The game was not surprising, considering their first shots were pretty well matched.

Laine stepped around her as they traded spots to throw the darts but he didn't step away. His body was so close she could feel the heat radiating off him even through the damn coat. He never touched her, but her body was humming with an electricity Sarah had not felt before. She waited as the server dropped off two more beer before she took her shot.

"Oooh!" Laine's sarcasm rang, when she missed her mark by less than an inch. "So close, but so far away." He leaned in to Sarah to say it, goading her. She aimed and squarely hit the pie shape that designated the eighteen, and then hit the pie shape for the nineteen. She beamed a smile at Laine. They had been tied pretty much the whole game but now she had pulled ahead.

She faced him with a cocky smile on her lips. She had wanted to say something goading, and witty, but all she was able to do was blink. Her body was incredibly aware of how close she was to him. Everything in her wanted to push against him, reach up to wrap her arms around his neck and wrap her legs around his narrow waist. Her fingers played with the loose cuffs of his jacket that hung off her. He was looking down at her, his expression still and severe.

He reached out his hand, reaching under his jean jacket and rested his hand on her waist, his fingers lying over her jeweled belt. She was vividly aware of the small space where his fingers touched the skin on her hip. The simple touch was so intimate her body began to heat.

She wanted him. Aching desire flared and pulled within her. Her breath came in slightly uneven gasps. He had made the first physical contact tonight, the first move and now it was her turn.

Unspoken questions hung between them. She knew he was waiting to see what she would do. To see if she was feeling what he was feeling. To see if she would advance or retreat. To see if she would follow through on the flirting. To see if she was a coward.

She stood for an endless moment on the cusp of a decision.

She took a step back. Her legs shaky. His warm hand slipped away from her hip and lowered next to his side. The disappointment was written on his expression, in the shift of his shoulders and probably echoed the feeling wrenching her gut. She stood still, staring at him; desperately wanting his hand back on her hip. She wanted to throw herself at him. But she held firm. A foot away.

"I win," he whispered. Maybe trying to goad her to come back. Maybe stating a sad fact. Maybe that was the game all along.

"That's not the game I was playing," Sarah said seriously, and swiped up the darts in his hand. She tossed one that hit the twenty, then another that squarely hit the bullseye. "There are rules." She lifted her eyebrows pointedly and stepped back.

"You cheated," he said without heat.

"So did you." She walked away back to her friends.

SARAH FEARED Laine would follow her and want an explanation for her actions. But she had none. She had no answer. She had run, plain and simple. But he had backed off and given her space for the rest of the night; but that did not stop him from casting glances her way as he mingled and chatted with people at the Community Center. Sarah had gotten tired of talking with Becca about why Laine was staring at her, so had left early. But she did not miss the calculating look Laine gave her as she left or the way it made giddy flutters dance in her stomach. But looks and games did not matter right now. She had to focus. She had a champion belt to win and records to break. She could feel Nan's legacy on her shoulders, and she would not let her down.

CHAPTER 9

$\mathcal{I}$t was still pitch dark outside, but Sarah and Bruce liked to get a head start trucking the horses to the Calgary Stampede. The drive was only an hour and a half, part of that being on country highways and the other half driving right through the city of Calgary.

"Ready for another one?" Bruce asked Sarah, standing outside her truck window.

"Willing and able." She smiled at him.

"You have the passes and permits?" she reminded Bruce.

"Yup, we are good to go."

Sarah smiled and pulled the gear into drive and pushed on the gas. She was leading the entourage of trailers and trucks. She took one final glance at the large convoy behind her and quickly ran an inventory through her head; the big old Western wagon for the Stampede Parade, the tack, gear and feed for all ten days. The miniature goats and chickens for the agriculture complex. Percheron to pull the wagon and do demonstrations in the big tent and of course the barrel racing horses. Her sweet Starbuck safely stowed in the trailer behind Sarah. And in the rear, the three trailers they would be staying in for the duration of the Stampede, right on the grounds.

The double-lane highways were quiet this early in the morning. They didn't meet much traffic on the way to the historic Stampede grounds in the middle of the city, where the Stampede had been held for over a hundred years.

Sarah smiled when she turned right and saw the large "Calgary Stampede" gate entrance welcoming everyone to the Greatest Outdoor Show on Earth. Her heart fluttered as she drove past the gates, giving the welcoming sign a little nod and turning back toward the barns where they would set up.

Her horses needed to settle in, and there was an incredible amount of work to do before the Stampede started.

Sarah couldn't wipe the smile off her face. The excitement for the Stampede was palpable. But there was something else rattling around in the pit of her stomach. She knew it was Laine.

EARLY THE NEXT MORNING, Sarah met with her friends and the other hands in the large stables. She could smell the sweet maple sausage and pancakes cooking on the skillet and her mouth watered. This was the first year she would be competing at the Stampede, but she had been in the barns shoveling, hauling and training since she was a kid. The smell of straw, hay and breakfast were a heart-warming and familiar tradition of the Calgary Stampede.

Pam, Becca and Sarah stood in the barns, happily eating the warm meal.

"Sarah, Carly said you really helped unloading her horse yester-day. She said you got her out faster than anyone has been able to."

Sarah shrugged. "The horse just needed a little coaching."

"Quin told me you got Delilah to stop chomping her bit, too," Becca added.

"When do you sleep?" Pam teased her gently, shaking her head. "I wish I had the patience to help other people with their horses."

"I wish I had the skill to be able to help people with their horses," Becca chimed in.

"It's not me." Sarah shook her head. "Nan's the one who knew how to do all that stuff. I just watched her."

"Watch. Do. Learn," Pam sing-songed. "And you have to learn from the best! You're a lot more like her than you think. You ride like Nan, you train like Nan. You even tell stories like Nan." Pam smiled.

"Tell the breakfast story, Sarah," Becca whined.

Sarah laughed. "The first Calgary Stampede was set to be one of the greatest spectacles the western provinces had ever seen," Sarah mocked, a grand storytelling voice pretending her friends had never heard the often-told story before. "They had planned bronc riders, and trick riders, and cattle exhibitions. They had sponsors and a location right here in the heart of the quickly growing city of Calgary. They planned to showcase riding and roping. Aboriginal communities were represented in their full ceremonial splendor. Women were able to compete. It was going to be phenomenal. But it was at the last minute the planners realized they had almost forgotten one crucial thing." She paused dramatically making her friends giggle.

"Community is what binds the Western heart. And what brings communities together?" Sarah paused again to shove a juicy breakfast sausage into her mouth. "Food!" she said around the meat. "And so, out of the back of an old chuckwagon, the first Stampede Breakfast was had. And people came by the trainloads, to an unpaved, newly budding city. And it put Calgary on the map. Well, that, and the flapjacks."

Sarah loved the tradition of the Stampede Breakfast, and even though there would be pancakes and sausages every day for the next ten days, she never got sick of it.

Becca smiled. "I love that story. Makes me feel less guilty for wolfing down three pancakes, 'cuz it's for tradition, you know?"

Pam and Sarah laughed at their friend, then turned as Bruce called to gather the Letters End crew and volunteers together.

"Morning everyone," he said, gaining people's attention. "Tomorrow is the Stampede. I want to thank each and every one of you for your hard work, I know it takes a lot to prepare for the Stampede, and you all put in a lot of hours. But with your help and continued hard work I KNOW this year will be one of the best!"

There were a few cheers and some applause.

"Before we finish our breakfast, I want to take a moment to recognize someone who is no longer with us, but who we miss dearly, Pearl Steele." Bruce paused and cleared his throat before continuing, his voice slightly more gravely than before. "I know she is looking down on us, probably wanting me to shut the hell up, and get on with it." Laughter interrupted Bruce, giving him time to grab a shot glass off the tray that was being passed around. "She always said all anyone really needed in life was a shot of whiskey and a kick in the ass. So," he said, raising his shot glass and the crowd around him did the same, "here's to you, Pearl." He brought the shot glass to his lips and swallowed the liquid. "Now get to work!" He laughed and wiped his mouth.

Sarah let the fiery whiskey burn for a few seconds before she tried to speak. Her eyes watered, from the effects of the whiskey, and the memory of her grandmother.

"You okay?" Pam asked.

"Oh yeah," Sarah said, brushing off the question. "That was nice what Bruce said, eh?"

Becca smiled, a girlish twinkle in her eye. "Do you think Pearl and Bruce ever had a thing?" she whispered.

"Can you imagine?" Pam whispered back.

"Nan was smarter than that." Sarah's voice was firm. "They worked together. That's all."

"Jeesh, Sarah, we were just kidding around." Pam gently punched Sarah on the shoulder. "Lighten up."

Her friends walked away. She swiped another shot glass filled with amber liquid and gulped it down. The burning made her cough.

"Whoa," Laine mocked, coming to stand next to Sarah as she coughed.

Sarah wiped her eyes. "I don't know how she drank this stuff."

"Ha, it puts a little fire in your step, that's for sure."

Sarah nodded. "Your trailer all set up?"

"Yeah." Laine nodded. "You?"

"Yup."

Laine had a fancy fifth wheel in the sponsors' section. It was nothing like her 1980 Scamper that was tucked behind the stables.

"You ate breakfast already." Laine nodded to her empty syrupy plate.

"Yup. Second plate actually." Sarah hated the stilted conversation. She kept with what she knew, work. "The Percheron will be loaded onto the wagon to head over to Fort Calgary to stage for the Parade. You gunna go?"

"Yeah." Laine kicked the ground. "Hey, you want to get something to eat tonight?" His eyes lifted to her face.

Her Nan had always said not to jump into a creek if you didn't know how deep the water was. Well, Sarah knew how deep his water was, and it was not safe for swimming.

"No."

"What?" His brows came together.

"Sarah." A skinny kid with jeans high on his narrow hips ran up to her. "Starbuck is kicking her stall and we can't get her to stop."

Sarah looked at Laine once more but realized that there was nothing else she could say. She headed down the stables with the kid to see to her horse.

～

IT WAS only minutes until the start of the Calgary Stampede Parade. Sarah and the crew had hitched up the historic Western wagon and the four large Percheron that would pull it. Early morning brought the familiar scents of horse and hay to Calgarians.

Her grandmother had lovingly said, Calgary was a combination of shit and steel. At the moment, with the skyscrapers towering beside her, and the large horses leaving behind steaming piles on the clean asphalt, Sarah truly believed it.

Sarah checked the straps and clasps to the bridle and harnesses a few more times. The four Percheron in front of the old, open-back Western carriage stood proud and stoic; almost as if they knew they were on display and they knew they looked breathtaking. A matched set in height, and coloring, their dark coats shone in the morning sunlight; they stood unaffected by the chaos happening around them.

The royal blue of their matching harnesses cast a stark difference against their black coats and brought out the phenomenal appeal that have followed Percheron for more than a hundred years.

As Sarah gently moved around the horses, fixing and petting as she went, she could not stop thinking about Laine. Darts with Laine had been a mistake. How she had treated him this morning had been a mistake. Hell, everything up to this point involving Laine had been a mistake.

She rested her head on the large warm solid chest of the lead Percheron. The horse responded, gently leaning his large head towards Sarah. She laughed a little and gave the gentle giant a scratch under his jaw. She had to keep a level head around Laine. She had to keep a level head. Period. Too much was riding on the next ten days for her.

The old Western wagon was painted black and had the same royal blue coloring as the tack of the Percheron. The wagon had a front bench, with a bit of a wall behind the bench to divide the driver from the passengers. The flat deck style wagon was decorated with Western heritage items, bales of hay and a banner along the bottom that read Letters End Ranch.

The marching band a few blocks in front of her started up and rounded the corner. Perfectly tuned instruments, a version of the Star Wars theme echoed in brassy beats off the skyscrapers surrounding them.

"Five minutes," the person in charge with a clipboard called out.

Sarah looked to make sure everyone was up on the wagon. She was pleased to see their excited faces looking around at the crowds gathered down the street.

She looked for Bruce, who was supposed to sit next to her in the front seat.

She felt the wagon shift on its springs and looked over to see Laine climb up. "Hey," she offered. But he didn't speak, just gave her a nod of greeting.

The band segued from a Star Wars theme into a Garth Brooks song in a seamless, horn-blaring transition.

The lady with the clipboard motioned for Sarah to go.

Sarah snapped the reins, the lumbering giant horses took a step, and without much effort the large wagon started down a closed main street of Calgary.

Sarah waved from time to time, but held fast to the reins. She was not feeling very Stampede-y at the moment and waving felt like a lie.

"Are we going to sit in silence for the whole parade?" Laine's question was a good one.

"I don't know what to say," she answered honestly.

The packed mass of people on either side of the road were waving, applauding and hollering a happy 'yeehaw'! Sarah usually loved every minute of the parade.

It was pretty spectacular that the entire city shut down its normal day-to-day business life to celebrate the Greatest Outdoor Show on Earth. Everyone here, whether they knew it or not, was supporting the proud heritage of the city with its deeply Western roots. That was something to be proud of.

The silence stretched until Sarah broke it. "You're my boss," she said, like those simple words explained everything, and in a fashion, they did. "Nothing can happen between us because you are my boss."

She glared at him. Angry that she had to lay it out so blatantly. She stopped talking long enough to pull on the reins gently; the four massive horses responded easily and took the corner veering to the right to lumber down another packed street of the parade route. When the team of gorgeous black horses and Western open wagon were on a straight path again, Sarah continued. "That means nothing can happen, okay?"

Laine leaned against the partition behind them, so Sarah had to twist to see his face. His expression hid what he was thinking but from his silence, she hoped he was getting her point. It wasn't enough that he heard the words, he had to understand what she was saying.

She had to ignore the butterflies, and the excitement and the draw of this man. She had to focus. He was her boss. She could be cordial and civil, but above all else, she had to be professional. She glanced at him one more time, her eyebrows raised, waiting for him to respond.

"I don't like it," he muttered like a petulant child. His arms were crossed, and his mouth pouted. Laine didn't move. There was a long silent pause before he demanded, "I want my jacket back."

The immature comment spoken so out of the blue made Sarah laugh out loud. Something shifted inside her. Maybe creating boundaries helped her relax. Maybe hearing Laine's pouty request made it less awkward; but her heart felt lighter.

"It's in my truck." She smiled at him, her attitude implying she would get it to him soon.

"It better not smell like girl," he said as he sat forward, leaning on his knees. His tone changed from the pouty child to slightly more lighthearted.

"It certainly won't smell like girl." She shook her head and smiled.

"And, just so you know," Laine said, his tone lighter, "I let you get ahead of me at darts."

"Bull shit!" Sarah called, though her smile lessened the impact of the words. "You were outta the running from the get-go."

She was thankful that the awkward silence was being filled. Even if that 'filling' was with Laine suddenly coming clean.

"And", he said, dragging out the word -she looked at him, an eyebrow raised- "I didn't like that you lassoed me." He said it matter-of-factly. "It was embarrassing. It hurt my shoulders," he said, "and my butt. I had to throw out that pair of jeans."

Sarah laughed. She was certain his intent was to lighten the mood, despite the honest confessions he was spouting. His intonation implied he was not serious, or at least not too serious about the wrongs he was stating.

"Are you done?" she asked when he was quiet for a few moments.

"I don't know yet. But if we are going to be friends, then I want to clear the air."

"You think we can be friends?" Sarah stilled and looked at him. The severity in his eyes held honest hope as well as an apology.

He shrugged. "Better than nothing." His tone came back to his regular, serious timbre. The joke was done, the mockery put on hold.

Sarah looked forward.

Better than nothing, rang in her ears.

CHAPTER 10

*T*he crowd sitting in the stands surrounded the infield. The rodeo was close to sold out and there was standing room only. Brightly dressed fans formed an almost encompassing circle around the dirt infield. But Sarah was only dimly aware of the people. She pushed everything from her mind to focus on the barrels.

Starbuck pranced under her, the horse's heartbeat thudding through her muscled frame. Sarah took a breath, deep and long. Letting the air blow through her nose as she relaxed her body. If she was tense, her horse would be tense.

The barrel was her target. She had to stay focused. One goal. There was no buzzer that rang, no countdown to make her go, everything waited on her.

Starbuck pranced sideways, her excitement building. She knew what to do, and she loved it. Sarah kicked, and the horse sprang into action.

Riding deep in the saddle, Sarah veered to the right, aiming for the farthest barrel. She hollered at Starbuck. The crowd roared with excitement. Sarah embraced the sound, it encouraged her attention-loving horse to greater speeds. She gripped the horn as Starbuck hugged the first barrel. She exploded around the tight circle and was off again. Sarah leaned far over the horn, encouraging the most from the horse. Four hooves pounded the ground in sure solid strides as Sarah came to the other barrel, yanking on the reins to make Starbuck turn. The horse didn't disappoint. She careened cleanly around the barrel. She hugged the edges without hitting Sarah's knees or knocking the barrel over.

Starbuck barreled toward her final target. Her legs reached far. Her muscles pulsed as she streaked across the dirt field to fly around the final barrel. Sarah yelled in triumph.

The crowd exploded to their feet and their cheers rose to a thunderous din as she flew across the finish line.

Sarah's breath came in heavy gasps that matched Starbuck's heavy panting. Sarah knew her horse's eyes were bright and alert; the little mare loved the excitement of the crowd and the speed of the barrels. A thrill of pride rose through her; for her and her horse. They'd done beautifully. Sarah walked Starbuck off to the side and waited for her time to be posted.

She tucked her hair under her hat and waved to the crowd. The cheering increased when her time showed up on the board. Sarah smiled, and gave Starbuck a much-deserved rub on her neck. She had performed well.

Bruce walked Sarah back to the barns where Starbuck would be pampered. Bruce was beaming. "Sarah, you were amazing!"

"Well, Starbuck was amazing."

The interruption didn't faze Bruce. "That's almost guaranteed day money. Good job!"

Sarah grinned triumphantly.

"Listen, I had the hands handle the stall cleaning and checking on the goats, so I want you to take tonight and enjoy yourself!"

"That sounds great, Bruce! Thanks." Sarah jumped off Starbuck. She could use a night off.

"Oh." Bruce had almost walked away. "Before I forget. Ashley called and said some lawyer stopped by the house looking for you.

She wanted me to pass on the message. They said they would contact you later."

And just like that the stressful ache was back in her stomach.

～

THE GIGANTIC HORSESHOE sign outside the bar perfectly matched the Western honkytonk theme. Sarah's boots stuck to the beer-spilled wooden floorboards, and the country music was so loud it hummed through her body and threatened to deafen her. She loved Ranchman's. Sarah headed straight for the icy tubs of cold Budweiser.

The bottle was cold, and she took a long swallow before heading towards the back of the bar where her friends would be sitting.

"Sarah!" Becca yelled and stood, raising her hands in the air as she approached. Becca swayed gently on her bar stool. Her white lace top hugged her body and matched the fit of her skin-tight jeans. "Where have you been all my life?" her friend yelled over the music and draped her arms around Sarah.

"I think she's drunk," Pam said, smiling, stating the obvious.

"You think?" was Sarah's sarcastic reply but she hugged her friend.

"You were phenomenal today!" Becca struggled to pronounce the word. "Man, those were awesome runs!"

Sarah laughed. "Thanks. It really was all—"

"Don't say the horse," Pam interrupted. "You always say it's the horse. But I can guarantee that if I rode Starbuck she wouldn't fly like that around the barrel."

"You just seem to know something... you know?" Becca looked at Sarah like she was holding the secrets to some conspiracy. "You would tell us, wouldn't you?"

"All my secrets and dreams, Becca. In a heartbeat."

Sarah's answer made Becca smile. "Good! Then I have something to tell you." Becca leaned in to whisper loudly to Sarah. "Laine Young is here with his friends, and he is looking fine!"

Sarah hated feeling the instant butterflies; the eruption of excitement was disconcerting. She shouldn't look, and she shouldn't want to look. She and Laine had an agreement at this point, their friendship was manageable. She should leave well enough alone. She knew that. But it didn't stop her from twisting to see where Becca had indicated Laine would be. She saw him.

Laine wore his typical dark jeans and belt buckle, but had on a newer plaid shirt, his black hat and a smile that made Sarah's heart beat faster.

"Right?" Becca smiled and nodded, noticing how long Sarah had stared at Laine. "His friend to the right of him is cute, too!"

Sarah didn't look at Laine's friends, she couldn't seem to tear her gaze away from him. He didn't know she was looking; she took her time devouring his masculine presence.

A tall skinny blonde strode up to him and ran her finger along his buttoned shirt. Sarah looked away. "I need another beer," she said as she headed to the back corner.

Sarah veered towards the women's bathroom between the live band crammed into the corner and the bar. She slowed her pace looking at the collage of history that overwhelmed every nook and cranny of the old Western bar. A saddle hung like a trophy on the wooden ceiling beams. Belts, buckets and skins were scattered in decorative homage to Calgary's Western heritage. She was fascinated by the homage to the barrel racers. A collage of amazing women riding incredible horses around low barrels.

Sarah moved a step and looked at the picture of Nan; it perfectly captured how remarkable Pearl was. Horse and rider were mid-turn around the barrel. Nan must have been in her twenties. Gorgeous, courageous and proud. Nan's cowboy hat hung low on her face, her mouth contorted, encouraging the horse. Her hands gripped the reins fearlessly as she rode the little pinto to victory.

The unmistakable connection between horse and rider moved Sarah. She felt the passion from this one poignant picture.

"You look like her, you know." Sarah jumped. The lowly spoken question jarred her back to the noisy bar. She didn't have to turn to know who spoke, so she didn't bother to look.

Sarah shook her head. "She was amazing, look at that control."

Laine leaned closer, his chest gently touching Sarah's back.

"What year was that?" He leaned closer to the picture, his body circling Sarah's. She inhaled, taking in his clean scent. His face fit perfectly between her shoulder and cheek, his large hat creating an illusion of privacy. She shrugged gently. "Early fifties, I think."

"Wow." He didn't say more. He didn't move. They stood there, her back to his front, facing the wall for a few intimate seconds. He smelled like soap and sunshine and pure man. Sarah felt her nipples harden and gooseflesh run along her arms. She tipped her head a little, feeling his warm breath caressing her neck.

"You were phenomenal today," he whispered, sending shivers along her spine. "You looked… amazing."

Sarah didn't move. She allowed herself to feel his compliment, and not brush it off, and not scoff at it. She let the simple pleasure roll through her.

She looked at Nan jockeying that barrel horse to the championship and something shifted in her. She didn't know if it was her win today or something else. Suddenly, she was sick and tired of being sick and tired.

The live band changed tempos and the upbeat twang of old-school country music made Sarah turn and smile at Laine. The smile he gave back, with his straight line of bright white teeth in his sun-darkened face almost took her breath away. She leaned into the feeling of abandon that the Stampede could give. The carefree feeling of living for the moment, living only once.

Sarah's heat skipped a beat when he gripped her hand and led her to the dance floor. She gave Becca a funny face as she passed her friends. Becca lifted her beer bottle and 'whooped' in encouragement.

The dance floor was bustling. Groups of women dancing in little circles, college students in flashy, slightly skimpy Western wear clapped while they danced, and other two-steppers twirled and dipped around the perimeter of the dance floor. Laine's hands were firm and sure as he gripped her waist and held her left hand higher. His big cowboy boots moved to the rhythm, his strong hands pushing and swinging Sarah like a pro. As Laine swung Sarah into a quick spin people took a step back, giving the good-looking couple space to move.

Sarah couldn't wipe the smile from her face as she was spun and dipped and hugged as Laine danced with her. Two-stepping was in her blood, she was two-stepping out of the cradle, but not a lot of men she ran into could actually keep the slightly awkward rhythm; step, step, quick quick step rhythm of the old-fashioned dance. But Laine, with his wide shoulders and tight jeans kept her moving and he didn't miss a beat. He was careful to not swing her into anyone else on the dance floor, which was also a nice treat. He lifted his hat as he spun her around his back and grabbed her hand to bring her into a quick spin in front of him, then dipped her low for the final twangy beats of the song.

They were both laughing and sweating when the song ended and the band moved into another fast-paced country song. "Want a drink?" Laine asked, miming sipping a beer in case she hadn't heard him over the music.

Sarah nodded and followed him as he led her off the busy dance floor back to her friends. He happened to catch a server as she passed. "Can I get a round for the table, please?"

The server nodded and disappeared into the crush of people.

"You two looked good out there," Becca said, tipping a bottle of light beer to her lips.

But Sarah could not wipe the smile from her face or stop glancing at Laine. He stayed next to her without crowding her. He was charming and funny, and attentive to her and her friends. But he did not touch her other than when they were dancing. Which made her ache to be touched by him. He was respecting her boundaries, which oddly made her want to tear those boundaries down.

He spoke highly of Letters End. She could see the ranch had captured something in him, something that perhaps he had been looking for here in Alberta.

"I have never seen anything like it." He talked loudly so the table could hear him over the band. "The clouds arched across the sky in this bright pink brilliant canopy. It was amazing!"

"It's called a Chinook," Sarah told him. "The warm wind that comes over the mountains causes it."

"It's really cool."

Everyone laughed understandingly. Sarah looked at Laine again as he spoke to her friends. She felt a pull of longing. It was stronger, firmer and deeper. Her attraction was more than physical.

The thought of possibly starting something with Laine Young entered her mind, and she almost dismissed it. Pam's earlier comments that Sarah was afraid rushed back. She was afraid of getting hurt again. Afraid to put her feelings on the line. She had been telling herself that she had to stay focused and had to keep her mind sharp, which was true, but she was a grown woman. She knew she was more capable than she was giving herself credit for. She stared thoughtfully at Laine.

He must have felt that she was staring because he turned to look at her. But he did not comment on catching her looking at him. He just smiled and made a funny wiggle with his eyebrows and continued talking.

Sarah almost smiled, too, until she noticed his expensive cowboy hat and new name brand shirt and jeans. Her faded Western wear was great quality but wasn't new or expensive. Her bills and responsibilities came to the forefront of her mind once more. Even if she did want to start a relationship, would Laine want anything serious with a woman like her? Did she want anything serious?

"Sarah!" Pam yelled and shocked Sarah out of her grim train of thought. "Are you thinking about the apocalypse over there? Smile for Pete's sake! This is our song!" Pam did not give Sarah the chance to object. Her friend gripped her arm and dragged her onto the dance floor.

Sarah wholeheartedly took up the distraction of the song, and the dance, and her friends. She let thoughts of bills and lawyers, and Laine wash away to the echoing twang of the steel guitar.

CHAPTER 11

*T*he next day passed in a blur of hay, dirt and barrels. Sarah got up before the sunrise to check on the horses and get ready for the Heavy Horse Show. She had to make sure the Percheron were groomed and their tack was oiled and ready. She was dog-tired after staying up late at the bar, but the well-being of the animals came first and always, so she hauled herself out of bed and got to it.

She was so busy with practicing and the animals' care, she didn't have time to worry about Laine, or debating or thinking about anything other than what job had to be done next. She devoted her full attention to her chores and practicing for the afternoon races.

Starbuck had been right on the money for all the races. She'd turned on a dime and ran like there was nothing she would rather be doing than racing at breakneck speeds to the next barrel. Sarah was thrilled with Starbuck's performance. They came within a fraction of a second of breaking the record. She was so proud of Starbuck's achievement, she couldn't stop smiling as she washed and then stabled the horse for the night.

Sarah was stopped a few times by other riders, who asked for her advice or opinion. She didn't mind sharing her expertise; she was happy to help. She even stopped at one of her competitors to show a technique of rubbing down the muscles in the horse's legs to encourage circulation and relaxation. It wasn't until the end of the night, after the rowdy, thrilling chuckwagon races were complete that she had a second to herself; and she knew exactly where she was going.

Sarah smiled as she made her way out of the grandstand, where the singing from a group of young singers echoed into the busy carnival and onto the streets outside.

The sun had set a long time ago, but the pavement still held the summer's warmth. Couples walked past her hand in hand, eating cotton candy and corn dogs. Children, who looked exhausted, ran in front of her, faces painted and chocolate on their hands.

Sarah smiled, taking in the intoxicating mix of smells and sounds. The ring and buzz from the carnival games competed with the laughter and screams from the fair's rides. The midway consisted of streets of vendors that held deep-fried deliciousness, beer gardens with live entertainment, and thrilling rides that twirled and flung their strapped-in, screaming passengers relentlessly.

She strode past the corn dog stand and made a mental note of where the deep-fried Snickers were, then headed to the Skyride; one of the only slow, leisurely rides, that was more like a chairlift at a ski resort than a ride. There was no line, she knew there wouldn't be at this time of night. She climbed into the ride's car and was just about to pull the lever down when a body landed next to her.

"Here's my ticket." Laine reached out as he pulled down the bar that sat across their laps, and then handed the ride attendant his ride ticket.

"What the—" Sarah's words came more from shock than from real agitation, to unexpectedly have a passenger beside her. She stared at Laine, mouth slightly agape, as the chair slowly ascended to start its relaxed trip across the grounds.

Sarah loved the Skyride. It was the first ride Nan had taken her on as a little girl. She could watch all the people and goings-on as she looked down onto the midway below, or out onto the city. The lights and buzz of excitement that echoed upward were as calming as they were exciting. The heat from the day had turned to a soft warmth that soothed and embraced her. Her feet dangled over the food trucks and masses of people.

She stared at Laine and worried that she must stink like a stable. Her hat was back in the barns, her hair a flyaway mess and her face must be streaked with dust and sweat from taking care of the horses. She wished she had brushed her teeth, though she probably smelt like the caramel apple she had wolfed down earlier. She pushed the thoughts away, Laine had seen and smelled her when she had been much worse off.

"Hi." Laine twisted to look at her.

"Hey," she said back. "What are you doing?" she asked, kind of pointlessly.

"I've never been on this ride," he said, looking over the edge. "Is it fun?"

"'Fun' is the wrong word. But I like it. I didn't know I'd have company. What's up?"

He leaned back, taking a deep breath. The small bench seat didn't allow for much room, so it seemed natural for him to lay his arm along the back of the chair as he turned to face her. "I didn't see you all day. And I wanted to tell you how great you did today."

Sarah nodded. "Thanks. Starbuck really brought it. Anticipated the turns, and didn't get lost on the way to the barrel, and she kept her head so low and legs—"

"I said *you*, how good *you* did."

Sarah smiled gently. "Well… it's a team effort."

"Becca said that no matter what horse you rode, you would still come away with day money. And that today was one of your best rides ever."

"Well, she's biased." Sarah smiled, wider this time, not immune to the praise.

Laine smiled back. His gaze wandered past her, probably taking in the large casino to the left with the cityscape as a glittering backdrop. A warm breeze ruffled his hair.

Sarah was very aware of his arm gently resting behind her. The warmth from it feeling hotter than it probably was. She squeezed her legs together and trapped her fingers between them, not sure what to do with her hands.

Laine was looking to the right now, taking in the large agriculture building, and smoke from the open pit BBQ. Probably seeing the large beer gardens with old live edged wood fences keeping the drinkers inside. But it gave Sarah a chance to gaze at him.

Her eyes fell, for some reason, to the muscles on his neck. The smooth skin there slightly brown from the summer's sun. His chest was broad, the blue plaid of his shirt lifted and fell evenly. Her eyes finally wandered to the dark stubble along his jawline. Then up to his cheek where a white scar appeared bright in the dimming light; she hadn't noticed that before. When her gaze finally drifted to his eyes she was not surprised to find him looking at her.

His direct gaze didn't embarrass her or make her look away. The edge of her lip lifted into something of a smile.

"Hi," she said in a breathy whisper.

His fingers brushed her arm, a light touch, almost not there, almost a tickle. "I missed you today." The truth in his words and his expression did something to Sarah's insides. She looked up at him, into his dark eyes that had become slightly stormy. She felt an energy between them, and electricity, too. The draw. The taunt. The desire. She wanted to move into his arms, and press her lips to his…

"I don't think we should be doing this," she whispered, never looking away.

"I know."

She wanted to lick the dryness from her lips, but all she could do was look into his eyes, her nipples tingled to life, hardening into tight buds. And the desire that pooled between her legs had her squeezing her thighs together again.

Screw it.

She twisted on the bench seat and slowly reached out to cup his cheek. The rough stubble there was a welcome masculine sensation. She tugged him closer to her. Her breast pressed against the side of his chest. The narrow bench did not allow her to move much farther, but she was able to pull his lips down to crush onto hers.

Laine's arms quickly locked around her, reacting to her need, and he met her lips with passion.

His lips were firm, and warm, and sent a pleasant rush through her. She sucked on his lower lip, taking it into her mouth and gently biting it before he pulled his lip back and did the same to her. Her tongue met his in an intimate exploration, making her spine straighten and her body push harder against him.

She moaned gently as his hand shifted to run along her arm and gently cup her breast. His strong fingers massaged the globe. His thumb found her nipple and rubbed back and forth, making her squirm gently again in the bench. She felt wetness between her legs and a deep wanting made her moan again.

Her hand explored the back of his neck as they continued to kiss. His hair surprisingly soft at the nape, his skin surprisingly smooth. Her hand roamed along his neck and slid down his chest, her fingers touching the buttons on his shirt as she slowly made her way lower without breaking their kiss. His breath slowed. She took pleasure in the way his breathing paused as she neared his groin.

She took her time, rubbing his flat lower abdomen, enjoying the way he sucked in his breath and pushed against her body. She finally allowed her fingers to press gently over the bulge between his legs.

He groaned as she cupped him fully through the dense fabric of his jeans. She moved her hands up and down his shaft and pressed her breast against him while she kissed him deeply.

"Getting off?" the ride attendant called when they were a few feet from the end of the ride.

Sarah pulled away from Laine and looked at the uniformed attendant for the Skyride. His youthful face seemed bored. Like he had seen this a million times before, but that did not stop the flush that crept up her face.

"We'll go around again." Sarah handed the attendant extra ride tickets, thankful that the Skyride's best feature was the return trip.

She looked at Laine as the seat rounded the corner to take them back across the park. His flushed face and glossy look told her he was also grateful there was more time on the ride.

"Well." He cleared his throat. "Wow." He adjusted his pants with his hands, taking his arm away from Sarah.

She licked her lips, missing the warmth of his arm, but understanding that the moment had passed. "Yeah." She bit her lips.

She glanced at Laine, who peered at the cityscape beyond and then at Sarah. There was a moment of incredible awkwardness, and then they both burst out laughing.

"Did you see the look on his face?" Laine asked.

Sarah laughed harder. "Did you see the look on *your* face?"

Laine laughed again. "I feel like a teenager caught by my parents."

Sarah giggled, then took a deep breath. Her body calming down and her mind more able to focus.

"I really did miss you today," Laine said, picking up almost where they had left off.

Sarah looked at him. The happy ignorance of arousal gone. But Sarah didn't feel regret. She didn't feel like this was a mistake. It felt… right.

Laine looked at her seriously. "Will you come to my trailer tonight?"

She looked out onto the Stampede grounds and took a deep breath. She wanted to say yes so badly. Her body craved his touch.

Her skin ached to feel his hands on her, and something deep in her core wanted satisfaction.

Which is why she didn't say anything. She looked at him. The Skyride sloped lower to deposit the riders where they had begun.

"Getting off?" the ride attendant asked.

"Thanks," Sarah said as she strode off the ride.

There was a mass exodus of people leaving the grounds through the south gates. The day's events were concluding, the Stampede closing for the night, but Laine and Sarah meandered their way through the grandstand, and back to the barns.

Calm settled over Sarah.

She didn't say anything, and he didn't ask, but there was an unspoken understanding between them. Sarah veered off from Laine heading back into the barns. She wanted to check the horses.

Satisfied that the horses were settled in for the night, and the nightly spectacle of fireworks hadn't bothered them, Sarah headed back to the far side behind the barns where some trailers were kept for the competitors. She didn't let herself think or talk herself out of anything. She held her thoughts and emotions in check and let an odd sexual determination take over her actions.

She pulled open Laine's trailer door, stepped inside and slammed it shut behind her. He stood in the middle of the room with a stunned look on his face.

Sarah didn't pause to think, she took the few steps that separated them and kissed him, grabbing his face in her hands to secure her lips to his. He stood motionless for a few seconds before he reacted; his arms moved to crush her to him and he deepened the kiss.

Sarah pushed herself against him, letting the pleasant sensation of her breasts rubbing against him combine with the tingle flaring between her thighs. She pushed harder against him. He staggered backward, something clattered loudly to the ground, but neither broke the kiss to see what had fallen.

Laine groaned as she gently thrust her hips against his hardening erection. Her body responded, and her vagina began to moisten.

Laine shifted. His hands gripped her shoulders and he tore his mouth away. They were both breathing deeply as they stared at each other. She could see the indecision in his eyes, she could see him struggle. And she was having none of it.

"I want this," she said, looking at him steadily, "I want you." She rammed her body against him again, taking what she wanted... what she needed. Her hands tangled in his thick hair and ran down his neck and back.

Laine's hands gripped her round butt cheeks and he dragged her over his erection, any hesitancy he had shown, completely obliterated.

Her hands reached down to tug his shirt from his belt and continued under his shirt to explore his smooth warm flesh. She gently raked her fingertips along his back, eliciting a groan from him as they continued to kiss.

She enjoyed the feel of his tongue as he thrust and explored her mouth, then retreated to allow her to explore with her tongue. She sucked on his lip then broke off the kiss to allow her to pull the shirt over his head. Sarah stepped back for a moment, the appearance of all the smooth muscle catching her attention. Her eyes roamed over him, taking in the barely defined six-pack, the lean narrowing hips and broad shoulders.

Her eyes traveled back to his face. He allowed her to take him in, the heat in his eyes smoldering as she reached out a hand and slid her fingers behind his thick belt buckle.

He inhaled in a sharp breath and she used the back of her fingers to graze the sensitive flesh below his navel. He reached out his hand to gently cup her breast. His thick thumb caressed the under globe and strayed up to push against the sensitive nipple.

Sarah pulled at the buckle and stepped closer to allow her hand full access as it slid past the jeans and down to grip his hard shaft. The fully hard penis was so smooth and so hard it made a full-out wetness gather between Sarah's legs. She rubbed her nipples on Laine's chest as he kissed her again.

She bit his lip gently and slid her hand out and stepped towards him, moving him backwards towards the bed in the narrow trailer. As she walked, she began unbuttoning her tank top. Laine unzipped his jeans. She slipped off her top and reached for the button on her pants. He used his thumbs to push his jeans and underwear off in one swipe. She unzipped her pants. Laine covered the distance between them and whirled Sarah around, so she fell gently onto the bed. His warm naked body was immediately on top of hers and his hands began exploring her curves.

His large callused hands searched her body, slowly rubbing up her arms, then down her sides. He slid her bra strap over one shoulder then the next, kissing and caressing as he revealed her smooth skin.

Sarah squirmed under him but let him take his time. She inhaled deeply when he undid her bra, peeling the satin fabric away. Her hard nipples perked firmer in the cool evening air. His groan shot a streak of pleasure through her and she whipped off her jeans, wanting to feel his naked skin.

He massaged and sucked on her breasts as his other hand gripped her hair. She kissed him again, pulling him over her, wanting him more and more.

He settled himself between her hips, her legs firmly wrapped around him. He pulled back to look at her. "I have to have you. Now. Hard," he said, posed to enter her, the tip of his shaft just barely touching her center. "And then I'll fuck you slow."

Despite his words he waited. She didn't know if he was waiting for her to answer, or to argue or to slap him. She had no words, her mind was consumed with wanting, and her body was demanding satisfaction.

She wrapped her hands around his shoulders and shifted her hips slightly; not waiting for him, she thrust slightly, allowing him to enter her fully. The full length of him sliding into her warm core in one smooth stroke. He pushed deeper, embedding himself and then he stilled. They lay there for a few heartbeats, letting the full feeling of pleasure and satisfaction radiate through them.

Sarah unwrapped her legs, and shifted under him, sighing with pleasure. Laine moved, the first tentative thrust was tight but every inch was laced with pleasure. He looked down at her, and brushed hair away from her. She shifted under him, the need driving her to rock her hips and search for more.

He was looking at her deeply, she could tell he was thinking of something. But she didn't want to think. She didn't want to know what he was thinking about. She wanted him to keep his word.

"You said you were going to fuck me," she teased.

It made him look at her again and his expression changed. He pulled his shaft out of her slowly, and thrust again, firmer this time, burying himself to the hilt. Then he did it again. And again, his hips thrusting in long strokes that were only slowly increasing.

His hand reached around her to grip her ass, squishing the round flesh there, then his hand moved lower on her legs, running along the smooth curves.

His pace picked up.

Sarah could feel an orgasm building. Tingling from her clit to her core, fighting for release. She cried out, gripping her fingers in his dark hair.

"Yes," she ground out, clinging to Laine as he quickened the pace again. She felt the pleasure radiate, an orgasm building in a wave inside her. She ground her hips against him, putting pressure on her sensitive bud. Her stomach muscles flexed, and her breath came in quick gasps.

"Yes!" she called again, her whole body tensing, her knees and toes tingling.

She cried out as waves of pleasure rocked her. She gripped Laine to her. The contraction of muscles in her vagina flexing and spasming with her orgasm. She could feel wetness cream out of her as her body pulsed around Laine. Her arms locked around him, her legs locked around him.

Laine increased his speed again, rocking into her, his muscled shoulders flexed around her, then he pushed up slightly, angling his body even deeper and he rammed into her. Sarah felt herself roll with another orgasm, less fervent than the first, but it had her body bursting with pleasure as Laine groaned deeply, his whole body tightening around her. She felt the pulse of his cock inside her and it sent a thrill of pleasure through her body. He groaned deeply, his body stilling on top of her. He held his own weight but nestled his head into the crook of her shoulder, his arms embracing her. They lay locked together as their breathing calmed, and their bodies cooled, and their heartbeats slowed.

Sarah felt his cock, less hard now, slip out of her. His face was so close to hers as he looked at her. His hand gently brushed her forehead, his eyes roaming over her features. Sarah watched him in the dim light; not sure if he was savoring this moment, or maybe he was too stunned to speak. Laine shifted to get up; his muscular back flexed as he scooted to the bottom of the trailer bed and got up.

Disappointment blossomed inside her. She didn't know what she had expected from this, but he was going to sleep with her and then take off? If he thought she was the kind of woman who slept with cowboys and—

Laine pulled a blanket that had fallen to the floor onto the bed and crawled back to her, lay next to her again. His arm wrapped around her as he made sure the blanket covered them both. His body pressed against her back, his legs to her legs, his chest to her back.

She was tense for a second before relaxing and snuggling deeper into his embrace. She wrapped her arms around his thick forearms and heaved a deep sigh. She could worry later about the list of things she had to worry about; right now, this comfort, this moment, this man... this was worth savoring.

Music from the Grandstand Show carried through the night, punctuated by the sharp blasts of fireworks. She smiled thinking of how they echoed the explosions that had happened in the trailer.

A relaxing calm embraced her. This felt right. And in this moment, she felt safe, secure and content. She snuggled closer to Laine, a gentle smile on her lips.

CHAPTER 12

*S*omeone knocking on the trailer door jarred both of them awake. Sarah stared at Laine, blinking a few times in an attempt to clear her drowsy head. The early morning dawn was just lightening the windows to the trailer.

"Laine," Bruce's voice bellowed through to them, "do you know where Sarah is?"

Laine stared at Sarah. She shook her head, not knowing what to say or do.

"Why?" Laine asked, raising his shoulders at her, mouthing 'I don't know'.

"She has an interview at seven and she isn't in her trailer."

Sarah smacked her hand over her forehead gripping the sheet to her chest. She had forgotten about the damn interview.

"Call her." Laine offered Bruce advice. Sarah hit him on the arm. He looked at her and whispered, "What?"

Sarah bounced to the end of the bed and began tearing through all the clothes on the floor, flinging jeans and tank tops and shoes.

A few seconds later, the jingling tune of Sarah's cell phone rang loud and clear inside the trailer loud and clear into the quiet morning. The vibration and song brought Sarah's attention to the kitchen counter.

She snatched up the phone and answered it. "Hey," she said, trying for a low whisper.

"Sarah," Bruce said from outside the trailer. She could hear him through the thin walls clearer than she could from on the phone. "You have that interview at seven, just reminding you."

She covered her eyes with her hand, embarrassment flaring through her. "Yeah," she muttered through the awkward moment.

"Okie dokie, see you there." Bruce ended the call, then banged on the trailer door again. "Got it. Thanks, Laine," he called unnecessarily.

Sarah knew Bruce would be laughing. And that Bruce knew she would be absolutely red-faced right now, which she was.

She looked back at Laine. He sat on the messy bed, with his beyond sexy tousled hair and smooth muscles beckoning her. She stared a while longer, taking in how attractive he was leaning back on his arms, his large foot peeking out from under the dark sheets.

It was then that she realized she had nothing on but her cell phone. He had been sitting there letting her stare at him, because he had been staring at her.

Her hair was an incredible wild mess, and her completely naked body less than sexy as she stood feet apart in the middle of his trailer kitchen.

"Come here." Laine's voice was low and gravely.

"Why?" she whispered.

"Because I don't want to have to chase you and drag you back to bed."

Sarah's eyes widened. The heat of embarrassment and a flare of desire conflicted with each other.

Laine flung the sheets off the bed and darted to the bottom in an obvious move to capture her. Sarah made a choice, and ran at him, knocking him back to the bed.

She lay on top of him, feeling his erection brush against her thigh. She laughed at him straddling him easily. She raised both her hands to gather her hair off her face. The move brought her breasts out and she reveled in the inhibition she felt on display for him. His hands cupped her breasts gently; lifting them and letting them down, enjoying the bounce.

She let her hair go and leaned over him. She kissed him. Her lips gently touching his, exploring patiently. The unambitious feeling of night was gone. It was the dawn of a new day, and things felt different. She snuggled her body on top of his, loving how rough body hair was coarse against her softer curves.

His hands gently held her hips, softly running the backside of his fingers along her side. Gooseflesh rose along her spine.

"Hi," she whispered as she brushed his face with her hand, pushing the dark locks off his forehead.

"Hey," he answered.

She shifted, spreading her legs on either side of him and pushing herself up again into a seated position. She shifted a little, letting the swell of his penis rub against the fold of her womanhood.

Good decisions could wait until later.

CHAPTER 13

$\mathcal{S}$arah stood in the middle of the barns, with people working in the background, and her horses' tails swishing in the cool morning air. She had pulled her hair into a pony tail and thrown on her hat; classic interview attire; and went to meet the cameras and interviewer. The interview was typical.

"What can you attribute your win to?" Melissa Faraday from Global News put a microphone in her face and the camera was a little too close for comfort.

"Starbuck, my horse. She was on top of her game yesterday. She loves to run, and there is no better place to run than here." Sarah pointed to the space around her.

Sarah focused on the questions, even though her mind kept wandering to the dark-haired cowboy she had left in his trailer. A smile tweaked her lips. She answered the questions easily.

After the interview, Sarah worked on the Percheron. The Heavy Horse Show had them working pretty hard yesterday and they would do well with some treatments and attention.

Her attention was split between the horses and memories of the tangle of limbs and intense pleasures of last night. Laine had turned out to be surprisingly tender, and sweet.

Laine had made her coffee before her interview and had told her she looked pretty before she left.

Laine had gently smacked her on the ass as she left his trailer and whispered, "Good luck." His simple comment left her feeling warm and cared for.

And the sex? Wow! She could not stop thinking about the sex. It had been amazing. Her body tingled just from thinking about it. But it was the quiet moments after sex, when he held her, wrapping his body around her, that sent soft warm feelings through her that had nothing to do with sex.

She didn't want to get ahead of herself, but maybe she had been too hard on him. Maybe there was more to him, more than she gave him credit for. Maybe she had been wrong.

Sarah's body ached slightly. She was used to being in the saddle for hours at a time, but after a night with Laine, she was feeling muscles she honestly had never felt before. She stretched her back and stepped away from the Percheron stall. They were ready for the Heavy Horse Show, but Sarah wanted to oil the tack once more, to make sure they had an undeniable shine.

She strode through the barns and heard Laine's voice. She veered toward the sound. He stood outside the stable in the sun, kicking a clump of dirt under his boot, his arm bent, a phone to his ear. Sarah slowed her pace not wanting to interrupt his phone call.

His voice sounded different, his tone not quite what she was used to.

"...yeah, a little redneck, hillbilly. Oh yeah, it's gunna take loads of funding to get it to the twenty-first century."

She didn't know who he was talking to, but his snide tone made her brows furrow. Who was he calling a hillbilly?

"No, not yet, but by the end of summer we'll knock down the main barn and get... yup, it's already in the plans." He booted the clump of mud again.

Laine laughed at something the person on the phone said. For some reason his laugh grated on her nerves. And set her teeth to grinding.

"Yeah. Don't get me wrong, I found a few perks." He laughed again. "You know me. Bag 'em and tag 'em."

Her heart dropped.

Sarah had heard enough. She turned on her heel and stomped away. Laine was talking about taking down the stable? About rebuilding it? He couldn't rebuild it! How can you rebuild a historical building? Rage bubbled inside her, and for some reason tears came to her eyes! She growled under her breath, her face contorting. She fought to control her rising emotions, but her fists balled up and she felt like she had to punch something.

She had been so stupid. To think he was serious about being with her. To let herself fall for someone like him.

She paused midstride. Fall for him? When the hell had that happened? Surely, she hadn't *fallen* for him? She wasn't that dumb, was she? He was a bull rider, and she knew how they were with women; she should have known better. She felt used, and disposable. Why had he even bothered trying to convince her he was different, when he wasn't different at all. Was it all just a game to him?

She gasped as she walked quickly through the stables, passing the horses and making a beeline for her trailer. Was she just something else he could conquer? A challenge to be won and then bagged and tagged?

Level thoughts knocked at her consciousness, that there was no way he could be like that, and that she must have misheard him, but his words echoed in her mind, 'bag 'em and tag 'em.' Rage muted any other thought.

SARAH KEPT the agitation with her for the morning. It accompanied her while she practiced with Starbuck. Later, she held the rock of anger with her as she raced, somehow managing to shave off a little time while tearing around the barrels. It managed to keep the joy from her eyes as she smiled to the cheering crowds. They applauded her almost record-breaking run. She wasn't happy with her second run either; as she spun around the third barrel, her knee knocked it and the barrel teetered on its edge. But she was angry enough to slam her hand over it as she flew past, stopping it from falling over, saving her from the five-second penalty and causing the crowds to erupt in near deafening applause. But her anger stayed with her. It had her veering back to the barns instead of answering interview questions.

"Bruce, I noticed that one of the Percheron has a swollen ankle. I don't think he should be used for the heavy horse expo tomorrow."

"Is that what has you in such a mood?" Bruce raised his eyebrow at her. "I thought you'd be in better spirits today." The tall cowboy smiled.

Sarah couldn't tell if he was joking or teasing her and frankly she didn't care. She wasn't in the mood for joking or teasing. "I'm sending two hands back to get Nigel."

"Sure. That horse would do anything you asked him to. But that means—"

"I know. I'll muck out the stalls, I really don't mind," she said as she walked away.

Sarah gave instructions to the hands to drive back to Letters End and get Nigel and then she headed to the stalls to muck them out.

Sarah really didn't mind. She had enough on her mind to keep her occupied as she heaved dirty straw into the wheelbarrow. Her mood was not fit to be in public. She grabbed the shovel and started working out her frustration.

"You did good today," Laine said from behind her. "But you do good all the time."

Sarah paused for a second, to let the shock of anger she felt run up her spine lessen and forced herself to use a professional tone. "Thanks." She continued to work.

He didn't leave. She didn't turn. Another shovelful of dirty straw went into the wheelbarrow. Silence stretched.

"You okay?"

"Yup," was her curt reply.

"Did I do something to piss you off?"

Sarah bent deep to gather the remaining straw into the shovel then hefted it into the barrow. She threw the shovel on top of the wheelbarrow.

"What are your plans with the old barn at Letters End?" she said, irritation in her tone.

"What?"

"What exactly are your plans? Are you going to tear it down?" She dropped the wheelbarrow and glared at him.

"Sarah—"

"What?" she demanded, glaring at him, panting slightly. Her emotions were unpredictable. Wanting and not wanting. And angry, but not wanting to be angry. She hated that she kind of wanted to cry and curl up in his arms. She smothered the feelings and glared at him.

"What?" she said again, emphatically. The depth of the question hung in the air, with the fresh scent of stable and manure and hundreds of unspoken words.

"Why are you mad at me?"

Sarah stared at him. Letting the words sink into her consciousness. Her first reaction was to scoff and keep walking, preserving and defending what was left of her, but she continued to stare.

"After last night…" his voice tailed off.

After last night what? She wanted to scream at him. *You thought things would change, you thought there would be something between us, you thought some magical moment would happen and turn the poor cowgirl into something the rich cowboy would want?*

But Sarah didn't say that. It was *her* misguided belief, not his. So, she went with the truth. "I heard you on the phone."

"When?"

"When you said I was a *perk*."

Laine shook his head. "I don't remember calling you—"

"Bag 'em and tag 'em." Sarah sneered.

The words seemed to jog his memory. "Oh, Sarah. I didn't mean…" he searched for words.

Sarah waited, wanting him to deny it, wanting him to assure her he hadn't said that. "I was talking to a buddy from back home. I didn't…" he scrambled a little more, then heaved a sigh. "I didn't mean for you to hear that. And I didn't mean it. Not like that."

"But you said it. So yeah, I'm mad."

"Sarah, I'm sorry. I don't think of you like that. I was just—"

"You were just what?" She didn't give him a chance to answer. "You were just behaving like your buddies expected you to? You say you don't want to be just another dumb bull rider. Then don't act like one."

She couldn't read his expression. Defensive? Pained? Angry? She didn't care. She had another issue. "What do you want to do with Letters End?"

He made a sort of exhale that sounded like a scoff. Confusion clouded his eyes for a second. "What does that have to do with—"

"You want to make changes?"

Laine's blue plaid shoulders lifted. "Yeah, so?" He seemed confused, trying to follow her questioning. "Sarah, there are new technologies that would make Letters End run more effectively. There is nothing wrong with it now but—"

"You're damn right there's nothing wrong with it."

"But in order to make money then some things will have to change."

"Letters End has been successful for years without new technologies. Even Nan lived without—"

"She lived in a shack with little to no amenities, that's not something to envy, Sarah."

Sarah's mouth popped open. Laine's eyes widened, also shocked by his outburst. Sarah knew he thought it, she had hoped he didn't, but this confirmed it. His arrogance and judgmental words shattered Sarah.

"My grandmother had more innovation and gumption than you will ever hope to shit out in your lifetime. If you understood, even for a second, the ability to give more of yourself than taking, if you even once put yourself second to someone else, if you had any idea what it means to value something other than money." She sucked in an angry breath. "But you don't, you can't, and you obviously never will. I happen to love my life." Her hand pressed on her sternum. "And I'll be damned if I let some city kid come in and talk shit about it." She gripped the wheelbarrow and stormed away from him.

She was so angry; her joints shook with it. She dropped the wheelbarrow and turned on him again. "Did you know my great-grandmother couldn't even own land?" Her voice rose with the emotions broiling inside her. "She had to marry a man to handle her father's estate because as a woman, she had no rights. And when her husband died, she lost everything. Women couldn't own shit. That's why Nan scrimped and worked and earned every penny so she could buy that *shack*," she spat the word.

Laine stood there, taking it. He didn't speak, letting Sarah continue.

"That *shack* represents everything good about progress. Throwing money at something isn't progress, it's gluttony. Nan worked hard so she could honor what her mother could not do. And she busted her ass every day until the day she died because she had the best sort of humble pride."

Sarah pushed the back of her hand under her nose to wipe the moisture collected there. "What the hell do you know of hard work? Honoring the people who came before us? You toss money at things. All you want to do is make more. But you haven't earned it. And when you're asked to stand up for something, like not degrading a woman you had been with to some friend… well, you can't even do that. It's the opposite of honorable. It's the opposite of proud. It's just plain pathetic. Don't throw coins at me, Laine. I'm worth more than you could ever compensate." She ground out the last word. Her throat tightened. She swallowed thickly. She turned and hefted up the wheelbarrow, pushing the stinking pile of hay with her head held high.

Laine didn't try to stop her. He didn't call to her when she left him behind.

She hated that she allowed him to hurt her. She hated that she wanted to cry. She increased her speed to get behind the next building, her hair whipping behind her and tears dripping over her cheeks.

She ran the conversation over in her head for the rest of the day, unable to get it out of her thoughts. She wasn't sure her rant had made sense. Could he even understand what she was trying to say? She didn't care. She told herself again and again that she didn't care. She had made one mistake. One night with him and that was fine. She had to move on. To focus on the rest of the Stampede and get her life in order.

She ignored the voice in the back of her head that mocked her, saying she had fallen for the handsome cowboy and she was reaping what she deserved. She was too upset to even hear the voice deep in her mind that said she could still be wrong.

CHAPTER 14

"Why did you bring Rouge? I told you to bring Nigel!" Sarah yelled at the two hands that had just pulled the truck and horse trailer back from Letters End.

"Bruce said he wanted a good-looking horse and we already have the wagon of Percheron here. I thought bringing her would really put some butts in the seats."

"Do you know why we did not want her here?" Sarah demanded.

The blank faces of the stable hands stared at her. "Because she's not ready!" She almost growled at the incompetent hands. "And what happened to the trailer?"

The long horse trailer was toppled slightly; the angle was not natural and it had Sarah bending to look under the trailer to see the problem. "The spring is broken on the rear axle; didn't you guys notice that when you were driving?"

The skinny cowboys scratched their heads and scrutinized where she was looking under the trailer. "Yeah, it felt a little wobbly, but it still drove straight."

Sarah wanted to smack these clowns. "That's why she won't come out of the trailer. She is not familiar with it, has little training in trailers, hates being moved and must have been rattled around back there for who knows how long. Dammit, guys!"

Thunder rolled in from the low dark clouds above them, in a deep rumble.

"Fuck!" Sarah swore. "Go get Bruce and get another stall ready." She had to yell the last after them as they ran to do what they were told.

A few raindrops fell. She could hear the chuckwagon races going on in the grandstand, the bellow of the horn followed by the loud fans cheering and then the thunder of hoof beats as the teams of horses flew around the half-mile track. She pulled her focus back to the skittish horse in the trailer.

Sarah pulled down the trailer door and walked in. The long three-horse carrier not only held the horses at an angle, but also allowed for the horses' feed, and contained a little hallway on one end. Sarah could see Rouge straining far inside the stall, perhaps hiding and seeking comfort inside the trailer walls.

"Hey, girl. It's okay, you're gunna be okay." Sarah used her most soothing tone. A shiver flexed along the horse's mane and twitched down her back, cautioning Sarah to pause. A warning.

She stopped beside the scared horse, not touching her, whispering cooing nonsense words until Rouge's strong frigid muscles relaxed. Sarah slowly approached again, using the small space as best she could to skirt by the horse, stroking her head, trying to calm her.

Rouge was having none of it. She shifted and stomped, not wanting to get out of the trailer. The horse huffed and shook her gorgeous head. Her tail was pressed along her backside and she searched wildly for an escape.

"You can't have your way, Rouge, you have to get out." Sarah could feel the charge in the air. The temperature was still warm, but the dark gray clouds that loomed over top were threatening to rain harder. Raindrops pinged on the metal trailer.

"Hi, sweetie, was that a long ride for you?" Sarah cooed, as

Rouge finally shifted her head. The fear subsiding as Sarah's familiar scent and voice penetrated the clouded thinking of the scared animal.

"I know, sweets." She stroked the horse.

The rain fell harder.

Finally Rouge relented, her shoulders slumped and her head lowered.

Sarah unclipped the halter from the anchor point and pushed Rouge backwards.

Thunder clapped in a vicious sharp uncontrolled sound that made Sarah jump from the force of it. The bright spark of lightning that followed lit the inside of the trailer and shocked Sarah's eyes.

Rouge bucked. The trailer and its contents shifted awkwardly. Rouge reared back on her hind legs and whinnied her displeasure. The whites of her eyes matching the white of her mane. Sarah grabbed for her halter, but the small horse was in motion. She jumped back and flipped around. Before Sarah knew what was happening, pain exploded in her rib cage, knocking the air out of her as pain blinded her. She was slammed against the wall, her face hitting the metal stall. She was almost crushed by Rouge when the horse shifted to try and get out of the trailer.

Thunder growled again and rolled through the clouds.

The horse's high-pitched panicked cries mixed with the low tones of the thunder. The rain continued to increase its downpour.

Through the pain, Sarah knew she could not let Rouge run wild in the barns.

She reached out, using the wall as a support. Pain made her double over and grab her stomach. She wanted to vomit. But pushed the thought down as she sidestepped the horse. The halter was just out of her reach. Sarah lunged to grab it. Luck alone made her fingers grasp around the rope. She tightened her hold. Held on. Rouge felt the restraint and pulled against the rope. Sarah was yanked half out the door. She knew better than to try and stop the horse on her own, but she also knew that she could not let go. Rouge pulled and shook, trying to get free. But Sarah hung on.

Somewhere in the back of Sarah's mind she knew that if Rouge truly wanted to get away, the much stronger horse absolutely could. But Sarah felt Rouge's fear far outweighed her stubborn determination, so Sarah continued to hold her and coo, speaking softly, firmly standing her ground despite the pain that radiated through her. The pouring rain drenched Sarah; she could feel her breath coming in harder, and it was getting harder to breathe.

"Sarah!" She didn't know who called to her, she couldn't bring herself to turn. She held fast to Rouge.

"We have to get Rouge to a stall," Sarah gasped, "she's scared. Put her next to Kitten, he'll calm her down." She clutched the halter, still trying to calm the horse.

Rouge stopped pulling and lowered her head, accepting the hold Sarah had on her.

"Sarah?" She could feel someone at her side.

"I just have to catch my breath," Sarah said, though her head was feeling fuzzy. The rain was soaking her and she had to squint to see.

"Sarah, let go of the halter. They'll take the horse to the stables."

"No, I'll do it, she's just scared and I—"

Sarah felt strong firm arms wrap around her and peel her hands off the halter. She didn't look, just watched as Rouge was led away from the trailer and towards the stables.

Good, Sarah thought, *she could get out of the rain.* Her eyelids felt heavy, and she couldn't help the weakness in her head. The buzzing sound in her ears. She leaned into the warmth behind her and her whole body slumped.

"You," she heard someone yell, "call an ambulance."

Who needed an ambulance? Sarah let her eyes drift closed. She would have to fix the trailer. "We have to fix…" She tried to speak, but her words came out in a mumble. She felt herself being lowered gently.

"Sarah, you're bleeding, and I think you're in shock." She recognized the voice, but didn't really care at the moment. "I don't want to scare you, but we have to get you to a hospital."

CHAPTER 15

*A*n X-ray, an ultrasound and eight stitches confirmed that she had abrasions on her collar bone, a bruised tailbone and two cracked ribs.

It hurt to breathe. It hurt to blink. It hurt to think. But nothing compared to the deep regret and pain of not being able to finish the races at the Calgary Stampede.

Sarah waited in her hospital bed to be discharged, glaring out the window at her rotten luck. The IV stuck to her arm had her lying in bed. They had to cut the clothes off her to complete the tests last night, so she was also waiting on Becca to bring her a change of clothes.

"Hey." Laine poked his head sideways into the room.

Sarah looked at Laine. She could feel the puffy swell of her eyes, and knew her hair was stuck to her scalp, so when he said, "You look good," she knew he was lying. Her heart didn't beat an odd staccato at seeing him, and she didn't smile back. Her face crinkled, and her mouth screwed up, and she started to cry.

Not silent emotional tears like she had earlier but racking sobs. That made her wince as she inhaled awkwardly. She covered her face. Wanting Laine to go away. Wanting everything to go away.

"Shh, it's okay, Sarah."

She almost didn't hear the softly spoken words. She cried into her hands at the hollow emptiness filling her. The pain of emotion and pain of her injuries threatened to overwhelm her.

A soft touch gently caressed the side of her face. She dropped her hands to see the watery image of Laine. His eyes reflected concern and affection.

She stared at him. He cupped her cheek and used his thumb to catch the trail of tears there, wiping them away. She moved his hand to hers, keeping his large hands in her smaller ones. His fingers wrapped around hers, gently squeezing them. His hand rubbed the soft flesh above her wrist reassuringly.

She sniffed. "How's—"

"Rouge is fine." Laine smiled slightly, apparently proud that he knew what she was going to ask. "We put her in the stall next to Kitten, and she settled right down." He looked at her. "I think she's worried about you, though." He paused and patted Sarah's hand. "She feels awful that she wasn't there to help you." His eyes dropped to their entwined fingers, then back up to her face. "She would have done anything to make sure you weren't hurt."

Sarah knew what he meant. She felt it in the way he looked at her. Understood it through their intertwined hands.

Sarah felt emotion bubble, a flicker of something light and exciting, but anger reared deep inside her; it stopped her tears and stiffened her jaw.

"Then she shouldn't have been the one to hurt me." Sarah's tone was harder, firmer than it had been before. She let the hurt she felt give her strength. This had to end. She knew it would eventually. She might as well cram all the pain into one big lump and let it fester.

"What?" Laine was, understandably, confused.

"What are you doing here, Laine?" She sat up straighter.

She ignored the voice in the back of her head that said she was being erratic, that she was not hearing him now that he was here and that meant something. That she was lashing out and being hurtful. She squashed the feeling and forged ahead with the easy emotion of anger.

She wasn't crying now.

Laine reached out to her again. "I'm here to make sure you're okay. I wanted to…"

She gave him a few moments to complete the sentence. She hated that she waited breathlessly, her heart teetering, longing for him to give something of himself.

She waited.

He said nothing.

"Sarah, I wasn't talking about the barn at Letters End, I was talking about my folks' place back in Manitoba."

Sarah wished she was more impressed by the comment, but she wasn't. "But you were talking about me when you said bag 'em and tag 'em?"

"I didn't mean it." He seemed sincere.

But that wasn't enough for Sarah. "We both knew what this was." She shook her head. "If I thought that you could put someone first before yourself, then we would be having a very different conversation. But your image, or your ego seems to come first. You have no problem being the handsome rich cowboy. And you don't seem to mind hard work. But the first time you have to stand up for something… for me… you cave." She paused as the truth of her words echoed through her soul. "We could never work out. I'm a Steele. We were never meant to be bridled anyway."

She turned her face to stare out the window. The sunny summer hills mocked the cold heartless sterile hospital room and the pain in her heart.

He didn't speak.

She didn't turn. She kept her hands firmly clasped together.

He stood.

Her heart cracked. But she didn't move.

She listened to Laine's boots slowly tread from the room. Sarah swallowed painfully. And her clenched fists shook. Part of her knew this was better to happen now, before it was too late. The other part of her wailed deep inside, that it was already too late.

"Okay, I have a change of clothes, and I was smart enough not to forget clean undies for you." Becca stopped at the doorway of Sarah's hospital room. Her cheeks reddened when she saw Sarah's face.

"Oh, Sarah, are you in pain? Are you okay? Can I get someone?" Concern etched Becca's face as she rushed toward Sarah's bed.

"I'm okay." She shook her head. Sarah wasn't sure. She was oddly numb after the emotional roller coaster she had been through. "All I know is I want to get the hell out of here." She swung her legs over the bed and began getting dressed.

Becca helped her get her jeans on, and gently pulled up her socks. Sarah hated that she was weak, but the pain in her ribs took her breath away. The doctor said there was nothing much to do with it but rest and take pain medication.

"There we go, sweetie." Becca helped her take off her hospital gown and slip a T-shirt over her head.

Sarah lifted her hands to pull her hair from her face but regretted the effort immediately. Pain stole her breath.

"Here, Sarah, let me." Becca gently, gentler than Sarah would have been, gathered up the dirty locks and pulled them into a loose pony tail.

"I asked Pam and Kelly to look after the horses until I take you home."

"I don't want to go home."

Becca's wide eyes gaped at her. "Where do you want to go?"

"It's championship Sunday. Take me to the Stampede."

CHAPTER 16

The heat of the sun beat down on Sarah in the infield. She looked across the dirt center where the barrels were set up, and then to the colorful mash of people filling the stands on the other side. The last day of the rodeo was usually sold out, and today was no exception. People who paid for standing room places were crammed on the tarmac in the hot sun to watch the events.

Sarah sat in the stands, next to Becca, and her heart ached. No. It didn't ache. It downright hurt. Sarah sniffed, trying to ignore the crush of pain and prick of tears in her eyes. The pain medication helped with her aching bones and muscles, but she wasn't sure there was a cure for the loss she was feeling now. Her ribs and tailbone hurt as well, but it was her heart that took the true beating. Pain meds didn't dull the ache for her soul.

The announcer's voice echoed in the stand, welcoming people and introducing the sport of barrel racing. "Many of you know exactly what goes on for a barrel race, but some of you may not know. Well, we have a surprise demonstration for you if you're not sure, and a little entertainment if you are."

Sarah's brow furrowed. The change in pattern was a surprise.

She looked to the barrel racing starting line and her eyes widened and disbelief filled her.

Kitten was standing proudly, calm as could be, waiting patiently at the start line. Laine sat on top of the huge gray horse. His black cowboy hat, blue plaid shirt and dark jeans made her heart pulse. The large horse made the cowboy look small sitting tall on the saddled heavy horse.

What the hell was he doing?

Sarah's eyes narrowed as she turned to Becca and Bruce who were sitting calmly next to her with satisfied smiles on their faces. Her eyes flew back to Laine and Kitten. She didn't know what to think. What was he doing here? And why was he on the horse?

He had a simple halter on the large horse, no bridle. His Western saddle was too small for him. But Laine sat there, waving to the crowds as he nudged Kitten into a trot and then into a quicker stride heading towards the first barrel.

The announcer continued: "Sitting atop Kitten, a six-year-old Percheron, we have Laine Young. Laine isn't used to this type of cowboying, he was the World Champion bull rider a few years back. But today, he has been kind enough to do this demonstration. No, men don't usually race in the barrel races, and yes, the horse is bigger than most barrel horses. But this will do the trick."

Sarah watched in awe as Laine guided Kitten to the first barrel and turned him around it. The horse responded to the commands but was not built for a quick turn around the barrel. The crowd laughed uproariously as Kitten knocked over the first barrel and trotted widely to the next.

"Now that would have been five extra seconds added if Laine had been participating in the races, but since he's just demonstrating, we will let that one go." The announcer laughed over the PA system, making the crowd laugh again.

Sarah didn't know what to feel, or what to do, or where to put her damn hands. She wanted to clap, and laugh, and run to him, and ride, and barrel race and nap, but all these emotions and desires just kept her paralyzed as she sat there watching the spectacle.

Kitten rounded the second barrel, without knocking it and the crowd went wild with applause. The horse swished his tail at the sounds but remained calm and followed where Laine was encouraging him.

The odd pair thundered back across the dirt center as the mass of spectators laughed and cheered encouragingly.

What did that mean? Laine had put himself in a ridiculous position. He must have known he would be laughed at, but he did it. He showcased the Percheron and rode around the barrels with his head high. It made the lump in Sarah's heart shift, and her mind start to think a million miles a minute.

Sarah watched the first barrel racer line up her horse. Her throat tightened because she couldn't be down there. The competitor in her screamed to participate.

She thought of Starbuck. The horse always stepped a little lighter and twitched her tail a little higher when it was race day. The horse loved and fed off the energy just as much as the humans did. Natural barrel racers, it was in their blood to want to run, and in their nature to want to accomplish. But Starbuck would have to be content to eat high-rated oats and hang out in the cool stable.

Next up was Pam. Sarah watched as Pam completed the cloverleaf beautifully and raced over the finish line. She clapped but only as loud as her hurt body and hurt heart would allow, her heart and her mind divided between being proud of her friend and thinking about Laine.

"That was awesome." She was able smile to Becca. Pam's time would be incredible.

She felt Becca's hand on her knee, giving her a reassuring squeeze and comforting pat. No words were spoken. None were needed.

"Sarah..." Bruce's tone was unusually somber, "...sorry you couldn't be down there."

Sarah nodded, truthfully devastated by not being able to race. She said snidely, "Yeah, I was really looking forward to the cash from winning."

Bruce looked at her oddly. "If you need cash, just sell a few Percheron."

Sarah looked at him just as oddly. "What Percheron?"

"Sarah, Pearl owned ninety percent of the Percheron stock at Letters End. You know that."

Confusion kept Sarah mute.

"You didn't know that?" Bruce said. "Pearl never wanted your grandfather to know, but she had slowly started to buy them and breed them. I thought you knew. Well, you must have read it in her will. What do you think she did with all her money? She wanted to make sure you were well looked after." Bruce gave her a little hug and looked back to the barrel racing with a satisfied smile.

SARAH BLINKED AWAY the tears that threatened, pulling a sour feeling deep in her nose. She was happy for her dark sunglasses, hiding her undoubtedly red-rimmed eyes. But Sarah knew if she let herself cry she might never stop.

Nan had one more surprise for her, and it made a warm, taken-care-of feeling blossom inside her. The manila envelope sitting unopened at her house flashed in her mind. But there was so much to process right now. Pain, confusion and sorrow kept her from focusing on any one thing. Her mind skipped from thought to thought. The fact that she wasn't down there racing made her ache. She had worked so hard to get here, she would have to work even harder next year to come back. Nan's gift cheered her heart. Then Laine's face echoed in her mind.

She sniffed again, not wanting to think of him. But his bright eyes and smile kept flashing through her mind; their time in bed, their time riding back at Letters End. How sweet he was while helping her making buns. His rough hands, his soft touch. His words echoed painfully, '*not much more than a hole in the ground, but it has some perks.*' She gritted her teeth as another horse careened around the barrels. The crowd collectively gasped as the number two barrel teetered and fell.

"Damn. Poor Cynthia," Becca murmured.

But the heart-crushing fall of a barrel for the other woman didn't stop Sarah's train of thought. What an asshole Laine could be. The arrogant cowboy that had tried to break a wild stallion. Who had been too stupid to get out of harm's way, so she'd lassoed him. The cowboy was goofy, and persistent and sexy as hell. And he had made a fool of himself riding the Percheron around the barrels. Was he trying to prove something?

Sarah clapped as another jockey flew through the cloverleaf and back over the finish line. Sarah tried to focus on the races. Her pride for the sport chiseled a small bit of hope in her heart as she watched amazing jockeys ride fabulous horses and achieve great times each round.

A black cowboy hat in the stands next to her caught her attention and it made her breath catch in her throat and her heart jump. But it wasn't Laine. Only someone with the same build. And the disappointment she felt then almost made her get up and leave.

What was wrong with her?

"Next up in your program is supposed to be Sarah Steele," the voice announced over the loudspeaker.

Sarah fisted her hands, digging her nails into her palms.

"Sarah is new to our Stampede family but not new to the barrel racing game. She broke two records barrel racing this year and was going to race today in the finals, but unfortunately suffered a few injuries. But don't worry folks, she is fine and well, but won't be able to compete." The crowd grumbled, the way that crowds do. "Sarah Steele comes from a long line of Stampede women, and barrel racing legends. Her grandmother, Pearl Steele, won the 1954

Barrel Racing championship and forged the way for many women and cowgirls."

The cameras had swung towards Sarah; she could see her cowboy hat and glasses on the large screen. Sarah was used to being put on camera from time to time but was grateful again that she was wearing her dark sunglasses. Becca waved, and Sarah smiled and waved as the crowd clapped. "Yes indeed," the announcer continued, "we have not seen the last of the Steele women, and we would like to officially invite Sarah Steele to come back to the Calgary Stampede next year, so she can have a go at winning the barrels then. How does that sound?"

The smile on Sarah's face was genuine as she nodded and mouthed a thank you to the crowd around her, and to the camera. The people in the crowded stands cheered encouragement.

"We hope you get better soon, Sarah Steele. The barrels will be here, waiting for you."

Sarah turned to Becca when the cameras were off her and smiled again.

"Hear that, sweetie? I am so proud of you!" Becca smiled at her friend, tears in her eyes.

Sarah smiled. Her cell phone vibrated; it was a text from Laine.

Congrats.

Three dots let her know he was typing. She waited to see what else he would say.

I'm sorry.

CHAPTER 17

*S*arah's heart was beating a heavy hearty thud in her rib cage that rattled her bones with the power of it. She sat in the stands gripping the armrests.

"Sarah." Becca's voice rang with expectation.

Sarah turned, wide-eyed, and looked at her friend.

"Go!" Becca waved her away. "Go to Laine." She smiled.

Sarah looked at her friend. "But what if it's a mistake?"

"So?" Becca shrugged.

Sarah blinked at her friend. Her answer was so simple. She thought of Laine riding Kitten around the barrels, putting himself out there. She thought of his comments at the parade. *Better than nothing.*

She was being an idiot. An idiot who didn't see where this could go. She attempted to stand, but the ache in her ribs slowed her down. She gingerly lifted her body out of the seat. She wanted to run down the bleachers and skip down to the ground level, but needed to hold onto the handrails. She made her way a few yards under the stands and stopped to catch her breath. What she doing?

She breathed through a stitch in her side. She hunched there, one leg tucked under her, her hand on her hip.

What if all he really was doing was—

"Sarah?"

She looked up and smiled. "Hi." She managed to get the word out, though her side ached. He was there, his strong arms holding her up. His gentle embrace folding around her. She couldn't lift her arms, but she wrapped them around his middle and hung on as hard as she could.

"I'm sorry," she said, "I didn't mean it." The relief she felt when he tightened his hold and murmured into her ear was worth the pain in her side.

"I know, Sarah. It's okay. You have nothing to be sorry for. I'm the one who was an idiot." He gazed down at her, looking into her eyes, probably seeing her spikey black lashes and tears pooling in the corners. "I know if this last little while has taught me anything, it's that I don't want to be away from you." He paused. "I can't be away from you." He searched her eyes for a response. "I am not a perfect man, by any means. I know that. But you make me want to be a better man. You inspire me to be a better man. I promise I was not talking about tearing down any barns at Letters End. And I never want to bag and tag you. And most of all, I think your Nan's house is the best home I have ever had the pleasure of being in. I don't know why I said it. It's not something to be proud of."

"Maybe because I was not making it easy for you to hold your anger," she said sheepishly at her own aggressive behavior.

"I don't want to bridle you, Sarah e, but I do want to ride *with* you." He was so serious when he said it, his voice was level, and his gaze direct. Sarah tried to stifle the laugh that came out, but only succeeded in making a choking sound that turned into a bright smile.

"I'm being serious," Laine complained, but with a smile of his own pulling at his lips.

"I know." Sarah tried to lift her arms higher, she wanted to circle his neck. She felt Laine shift and gently lift her arms around his neck, holding her hands in his again. "I know," she said again. More serious now.

They looked into each other's eyes, and the smile, and hope and promise they both saw there had them embracing closer, under the shade of the infield at the Calgary Stampede.

As Sarah kissed Laine she could hear the stands erupt in applause. She could hear the loudspeakers as they doled out the awards for Barrel Racing.

Laine pulled away suddenly and swore. "Shit."

"What?" She was confused and watched as he stepped away from her and jogged across the pavement to a security guard on a little white golf cart.

Sarah was a little shocked when the security guard got out and Laine drove over to her. "Sarah, get in."

"But Laine—"

"Just trust me. Get in."

His eager face convinced her, and she gently slid her bruised body inside the golf cart.

Laine drove quickly around the grandstands, maneuvering around the people strolling in the grasses. He veered this way and that until he had finally made it to the other side, where the stage was full of flag holders, barrel racers and announcers.

"What the he—"

"The next award," the announcer said, speaking into the ball of black fuzz on his microphone, "is a new one for us here at the Calgary Stampede."

A tall woman with long blonde hair and large headphones ran towards the cart.

She covered the microphone piece that bent around her mouth and asked, "Are you Sarah e?" At Laine's nod and Sarah's blank look, the blonde escorted Sarah onto the stage.

"This award is in recognition of an individual who has exhibited outstanding horsemanship. Devotion to the care and stewardship of animals. Has proven to be an educated mentor and teacher. And has unanimously been voted by the Barrel Racing community as most valuable. The LaDue Achievement Award goes to our very own, Sarah e."

Sarah accepted the large gold belt buckle with tears shining in her eyes.

"Your grandmother would be proud," the male announcer whispered to her.

Sarah smiled at the cheering crowd, grateful, humbled and truly thankful for the award.

CHAPTER 18

"Hey, what are you doing?" Laine asked, carefully sitting next to Sarah, not wanting to jar her as he sank down onto the couch at her house.

She didn't answer as she opened the scrapbook. The familiar scent and sound of aged pages had her sighing. She reached beside her for the picture she had printed. The one of her and Laine standing in front of Kitten. Laine's arm was holding the reins of the large barrel-chested horse, and Sarah held out her sparkly buckle from the Stampede.

The picture captured the moment perfectly; reflecting the color of the rich dirt, the bright white of the fences surrounding the infield and the vivid blues of the summer sky. The white and gray horse stood elegantly behind them; his large head facing the camera gave a stunning contrast to Laine's red shirt, and the dark blues of Sarah's plaid. The large belt buckle that Sarah gripped in her hands in front of her shone brightly, the intricate designs difficult to see, but the importance of the buckle was underscored by Sarah's grip on the reward. The picture was glossy, fresh, and new, the colors bright and distinct.

Sarah wiped glue along the back of the photo and pressed it

into the last page of the scrapbook. It felt like a piece of her fell into place. And even though her ribs hurt, and her eyes were puffy from crying, she felt safe and comfortable. She closed the scrapbook and wrapped her arms around the large album as she leaned against the warm strong chest of Laine. His arms gently wrapped around her, his large hands resting over hers. He leaned his head closer to her, tipping his tousled hair to rest gently against her.

She felt him inhale gently. And exhale. Just short of a sigh. She knew how he felt, and if she could inhale without aches in her ribs, she probably would have echoed his sentiment.

He shifted to allow his lips to kiss the side of her head, the motion slow and kind. The arrogant bronc riding cowboy had a soft and caring side. And apparently there was a soft side to a e as well.

Love the novel you just read?
Your opinion matters.

Review this book on your favorite book site, review site, blog, or your own social media properties, and share your opinion with other readers.

Thank you for taking the time to write a review for me!

WOMEN OF STAMPEDE SERIES

Saddle up for the ride! The Women of Stampede will lasso your hearts! If you love romance novels with a western flair, look no further than the Women of Stampede Series. Authors from Calgary, Red Deer, Edmonton and other parts of the province have teamed up to create seven contemporary romance novels loosely themed around The Greatest Outdoor Show on Earth... the Calgary Stampede. Among our heroes and heroines, you'll fall in love with innkeepers, country singers, rodeo stars, barrel racers, chuckwagon drivers, trick riders, Russian Cossack riders, western-wear designers and bareback riders. And we can't forget our oil executives, corporate planners, mechanics, nursing students and executive chefs. We have broken hearts, broken bodies, and broken spirits to mend, along with downed fences and shattered relationships. Big city lights. Small town nights. And a fabulous blend of city dwellers and country folk for your reading pleasure. Best of all, hearts are swelling with love, looking for Mr. or Miss Right and a happily ever after ending. Seven fabulous books from seven fabulous authors featuring a loosely connected theme—The Calgary Stampede.

WOMEN OF STAMPEDE BOOKS

Hearts in the Spotlight, Katie O'Connor

The Half Mile of Baby Blue, Shelley Kassian

Saddle a Dream, Brenda Sinclair

Eden's Charm, C.G. Furst

Unbridled Steele, Nicole Roy

Betting on Second Chances, Alyssa Linn Palmer

Trick of the Heart, Maeve Buchanan

ABOUT NICOLE ROY

 Nicole Roy is a proud Alberta girl who loves to tell stories. She lives with the absolute love of her life in a small town in southern Alberta, Canada. When asked what she wants to be when she grows up, she promptly says "who wants to grow up?"

She has trotted the globe, from Kenya to Croatia, Laos to Turkey, and writes everything from historical regency romances to contemporary sci fi. If her travels have taught her anything, it's that no matter where you are or how you got there (the good, the bad, and the unforgettable), it always comes down to people. Character is the thing, in life and in the story.

Visit her website at www.nicolebroy.com.

88991398R00095

Made in the USA
Lexington, KY
21 May 2018